S0-AGK-738

Alan stared at the beautiful, strange woman in his yard and then at the gate.

He'd opened it himself, once, with great difficulty. Somehow the petite woman had reached over the top of an eight-foot-high gate and pushed back the bolt. Clearly, she was resourceful, which was one of the criteria he'd stipulated for a nanny.

"The agency sent you?" He wished he'd remembered to shave. "I asked for someone older and—"

She made things much worse by smiling, a totally captivating smile that did odd things to his ability to draw breath. "I'm older than I look," she said. "Much older."

"No, it just won't do."

"You mean *I* won't do. Do you fear for your virtue?"

"My virtue?" He stared at her feeling incredibly stupid and awkward and oafish. To say nothing of unshaven.

She crossed her heart. "I promise not to molest you." She laughed. As it bubbled forth, he could hear nothing else, think of nothing else.

This was the nanny? He was in big trouble....

Dear Reader,

You face the eternal question that has plagued womankind throughout the ages: you're trapped on a desert island with one man. You choose: (a) Sylvester Stallone (b) Daniel Day-Lewis or (c) Tom Hanks.

Upon serious reflection, you may consider: Sly might be able to tear down trees with his bare hands and strap together a raft out of jungle vines but you wonder—what are you going to talk about? Daniel will look really, really good and want to discuss deep, philosophical issues at great length but all you can think about is does he ever lighten up? If you pick Tom Hanks because he's smart and handsome and charming and *funny*—then have we got the books for you!

LOVE & LAUGHTER—a look at the lighter side of love. With our inspiration ranging from the beloved screwball comedies of yesterday to the romantic comedies of today, we searched high and low, far and wide, just about everywhere, in fact, for authors who love and write romance and comedy. The results, if we dare be so immodest, have been absolutely fabulous.

We are pleased to welcome longtime Loveswept author Judy Griffith Gill into the LOVE & LAUGHTER lineup. *There's Something About the Nanny...* combines all the best elements of romantic comedy with a little dash of magic. Carrie Alexander, a RITA nominee for Best First Book, harks back to the screwball comedies of yesterday in a delightful romp. April Pierce, *The Madcap Heiress*, will steal your hearts as quickly as she does the hero's!

With love—and laughter!

Malle Vallik

Malle Vallik
Associate Senior Editor

THERE'S SOMETHING ABOUT THE NANNY...

Judy Griffith Gill

THERE'S SOMETHING ABOUT THE NANNY...

Harlequin Books

TORONTO • NEW YORK • LONDON
AMSTERDAM • PARIS • SYDNEY • HAMBURG
STOCKHOLM • ATHENS • TOKYO • MILAN
MADRID • WARSAW • BUDAPEST • AUCKLAND

ISBN 0-373-44007-3

THERE'S SOMETHING ABOUT THE NANNY...

Copyright © 1996 by Judy Gill

This edition published by arrangement with Harlequin Books S.A.

Printed in U.S.A.

Judy Griffith Gill, a resident of British Columbia, Canada, is the author of over twenty-five novels. She takes pride in writing about that age-old delight, falling in love. She says that when it comes to love, the two people involved have to be able to laugh together. "It's those dumb things that make a romance memorable to me—the characters trying to hide from themselves, from each other, from the world, just how deeply involved their emotions are. It puts them into awkward, idiotic situations and gives them something to laugh about together for the next fifty years."

For Fred Kerner.
Thanks for the vote of confidence.
The fullness of time is now.

1

ALAN MAGNUS PROPPED his elbows on his desk, dropped his head into his hands and groaned. He had the Monday Blues. His writing wasn't going anywhere, and it damn well *had* to. This final draft was due on his editor's desk in two short weeks. It had been scheduled months ago—long before the arrival of Deanna—and he'd blow his professional reputation, to say nothing of his self-respect, if he didn't come through as promised.

One megawhack of copies had been presold thanks to the publisher's sales reps' pitching his breakout thriller to booksellers as "out-Grishaming Grisham" and as "a Clancy techno blockbuster." It was a lot of hype to live up to—as his struggles to complete these final revisions were proving to him on a daily basis.

It was just as hard, if not harder, to have suddenly become the sole support for the four-year-old daughter he'd not so much as known existed until last February. He heard the back door slam as she went out into the yard to her swing-set, her sandbox and her solitary play. He would not look. He must not look. If he did, he'd find himself outside pushing her swing, or helping her build roads in the sand, or catching her when she swooped down the slide, pale hair flying, blue eyes dancing, a big, trusting smile on her face as she shot into his arms.

What he had to do was to get his fingers on his keyboard and finish these frustrating revisions.

Deanna was all right. He knew that. Yet guilt over her loneliness gnawed at him.

SPOTTING HER RED BALL in the long grass beside the fence, Deanna hopped off her swing and ran to get it. She threw it really, really high, hoping it would go over the fence into the yard next door. Then maybe someone would open the gate to give it back to her and she'd find out there were kids over there. It bounced off the fence. She threw it again. She wished she didn't have to wait a whole year for kindergarten. Daddy said maybe she could go to preschool. He'd see about it. But she thought he'd forgotten.

Daddy forgot lots of things. Yesterday he even forgot lunch until she got so hungry she had to ask him. He'd said again he sure as hell hoped the agency came up with a decent nanny soon and that's when she told him she didn't want a nanny because they smelled almost as bad as billies and said "ma-a-aa" all the time.

Daddy had put his hands over his face and said, "Oh, hell!" and then he'd said that the kind of nanny he'd get for her wouldn't be a goat. She might well turn out to be a dog, but certainly not a goat.

Deanna said that she'd like to have a dog, a little puppy, and he'd said, "Hell, no!" She'd told him *hell* was a bad word, and he'd said that he knew lots worse but was restraining himself. Then he explained that the nanny he hired would be a lady, not an animal. But she didn't like any of the ladies who'd come so far.

She threw the ball and it went way, way high, hit the fence right up by the top, flew away... and then didn't come down again. She gazed up at where it had gone—

into the apple tree. It was stuck. She lay on her back on the grass and stared up, wishing the ball back down. Lonnie, back at the farm with Grandma and Grandpa Hoover, said if you wished hard enough for things they might happen. She'd wished real hard and her mommy didn't come back, but her daddy came and got her, so maybe wishing had sort of worked.

A dragonfly buzzed by her head, its wings all sparkly like a fairy's. She rolled over, propped her chin on her hands and watched it check out some tall purple flowers, then it flew up to the branches of the apple tree where her ball was stuck. She wished it really was a fairy and she could ask it to get her ball down for her. What if she had a fairy of her very own? Wouldn't that be fun? The fairy could be her friend, too, and play Barbies with her and—

"That's it!" she cried, springing to her feet. "I can make a fairy!"

WHAT TO USE for wings . . .

Deanna rummaged through her toy box. One of her Barbies had long, golden hair, just like a fairy. She found a pink dress that would do for a fairy. It should have a frilly skirt with lots of petticoats but she could pretend that. But wings. You couldn't just pretend wings. They had to be real or the fairy couldn't fly. There was nothing in her room that would do.

She peeked into Daddy's office, saw the little moving dots on his screen that meant he was thinking. He wouldn't want her to talk, so she didn't. She tiptoed away and into the kitchen. Taking an apple out of a bowl on the table, she bit into it. Juice run down her chin and dripped on to one knee in muddy streaks as she squatted and looked in all the bottom cupboards where there was nothing but pots and dishes. She wiped her chin with the back of her hand, wiped her knee with the back of the other and climbed up on a stool and then onto the counter to peek in to the top cupboards.

Macaroni. Grandma got sick once and the lady at the next farm took her to play with her kids. They were big, and one girl had helped her make a picture of angels out of macaroni and glue, but she didn't think that would be the answer today because it wasn't a picture she wanted to make. Still, that window stuff on the front of the box looked almost like dragonfly wings. Or fairy wings. Back on the stool. she pulled open a drawer to look for scissors, but all she could find were knives. She wasn't allowed to used big knives, but a little one would be okay, wouldn't it?

Deanna stabbed carefully at the edge of the fairy-wing stuff in the box, then stabbed harder and suddenly macaroni pieces rained all over the counter, the stool and the floor, making a big mess and a lot of noise and bringing Daddy running from his computer and his book.

Deanna stuffed the knife behind her back and stared at Daddy, who stared back at her, then down at all the macaroni and shook his head slowly from side to side. "What," he asked, sounding very polite, "are you doing, Deanna?"

She told him.

He shook his head again. "Out of macaroni?" Now he sounded like he was trying not to shout. Grandpa used to shout and scare her and make her cry.

Deanna tried not to cry, but felt her chin wiggling in a way she couldn't stop. She sniffed because her nose started to run and her eyes were getting watery. "I needed the fairy paper from the box. I was trying to be careful, Daddy, but I could only use a little knife and it didn't work very well and all the macaroni jumped out. I'm s-sorry."

"Oh, honey, it's all right. We'll get a broom and clean it up. Don't cry, baby. Come here."

He scooped her off the stool and held her against his shoulder, rubbing her back and rocking her from side to side. Deanna loved it when Daddy did that. He smelled good. She hung onto his neck wishing he'd never put her down, but he did, of course, and got a broom and cleaned up the mess. He let her hold the dustpan.

"What's fairy paper, Dee?"

She showed him, and showed him the Barbie with the yellow hair and the pink dress. "She needs wings right here so she can be a real fairy and fly up into the apple tree to get my red ball down."

Daddy frowned and took bread and peanut butter out of the cupboard to make sandwiches for lunch. "Why didn't you ask me to get your ball down?"

"Because you were working."

"But I—" He slapped the lid back on the peanut butter jar. "Yeah. Okay. Guilty as charged." He stood very straight and tall, bent his arm with his elbow sticking out and put his fingertips against his eyebrow for a minute. "I'll get on it right away, chief. After lunch."

Deanna giggled because he looked funny. Daddy talked kind of funny sometimes, too, but she liked it. It made her laugh. She liked the way laughing made her tummy feel inside. She and Daddy did a lot of laughing when he wasn't busy working. Maybe when he finished his book he'd play with her all the time. She wanted him to get it all done fast.

"You can go back to work, Daddy. My fairy will fly up and get my ball. Just as soon as I make her some wings."

He hugged her again. "No, I don't think so, sweetheart. Better if I do it. That's what dads are for, you know, getting stuff out of trees for their little girls." He handed her a sandwich. They walked outside together, munching on their lunch, and he reached up into the tree and got her ball down.

Sitting on the corner of her sandbox with his knees sticking up all big, he said, "Fairies aren't real, you know, Dee."

Deanna laughed and dug her toes into the warm sand. "Sure they are, Daddy. They have wings and pretty dresses and they make wishes come true."

"Really." He looked interested. "If you had a fairy to give you wishes, what would you wish for?"

She thought about it a minute. "A mommy." Daddy said nothing, but his mouth made a funny shape. "Angels and fairies are sort of the same, aren't they, Daddy? Grandma said my mommy was a angel now and Grandpa said, 'Not before time, either,' and Grandma told him to hush. Did you know I had a mommy once?"

Daddy stared at his knees awhile and nodded. "Yeah. I knew that, Dee." Then he looked at her again. "Wouldn't a nanny do just as well?"

"Not as well as a mommy. Mommies read stories and stuff, and play." She tried to remember for sure. "I think, but maybe I just dreamed that. Grandma said I dreamed a lot of stuff and she wanted me to forget about it."

Daddy sighed and smiled all at the same time. "I think you remember right. I'm sure your mommy read

to you, and played, I don't want you to forget about it."
He made a growly sound and looked at the sky. "Why
can't that damned agency come through? They keep
sending me kids hardly out of diapers. Where are all the
good, old-fashioned grandmotherly kind of nannies?"

Deanna knew *damn* was another bad word but didn't
tell Daddy. "I don't want a grandma nanny," she said
in some alarm. "Couldn't we get someone nice?"

"Sweetheart, there are grandmas, and then there are
grandmas. Grandma Jan's nice, isn't she?" Deanna
nodded eagerly. She did like her Grandma Jan, who
said she was Daddy's mom. "And we won't get a nanny
who's not nice," Daddy said. "I promise. She'll play
with you, and read you stories, and take you to the park
and . . . everything."

"Still," she said, jumping up, "if I can't have a mom,
I'd rather have a fairy. Will you help me glue wings on
Barbie?"

Daddy sighed and swallowed the last bite of his
sandwich. "Sure, sweetheart. Let's do that now, before nap time."

ALAN SAT on the side of her bed, watching Deanna
sleep. He touched her petal-soft cheek and gazed at her
in rapt amazement. How was it possible that the first
three and a half years of her life had passed without his
so much as suspecting her existence? Shouldn't some
kind of instinct have told him? He and her mother,
Pippa, had known each other for only a brief, if phys-
ically intense, time, and then, one morning, she was
gone. Just like that. He'd tried to find her, questioned
the people he thought were their mutual friends, but
discovered no one knew her well, no one knew where
she'd come from, where she might have gone. Or why.

Then had come the letter, with a whiff of her scent and a blurred postmark. In it, she said that though they'd had fun, it was time to move on. She'd never forget, but she hoped he would. There was someone better for him waiting in the wings.

Wings. He touched the awkward cellophane wings he'd helped Deanna fashion and glue to her Barbie's dress. If he was a really *good* father, he figured he'd go out and buy her a proper fairy costume for her doll, but he had a deadline to meet and the past five months, adjusting to fatherhood and sharing his home with a not-quite-four-year-old, had put him way behind schedule.

Rising, he went back to his computer, secure in the knowledge that Deanna would sleep for another hour or two, and for that period, at least, he could quit worrying about her.

Raising a child was a huge responsibility. Raising one alone, a daunting task he had never once contemplated in his wildest fantasies. Until he knew he had a daughter. Then, there'd been no question but that he'd honor her mother's wishes and go get her. "Rescue" her, Pippa's final and unexpected letter had said. *Rescue...* The choice of word had been no accident.

DEANNA WOKE from her nap and smiled at the fairy in her hand. One wing was a little bit crushed, but that wouldn't matter. Fairies were magic. They could fly even with rumpled wings. Rising quietly so as not to disturb Daddy, who was working again—she could hear the comforting tickety-tickety-tick of his computer keys floating up the stairs toward her bedroom—she went to the bathroom, then slipped downstairs and outside with her fairy. Swinging her arm back, she flung the fairy aloft, watching its wings flutter and shine just like the dragonfly's. It flew into the apple tree . . . and stayed.

She jumped and clapped her hands with glee. "Okay, fairy, you can come down now."

The fairy just lay there on its tummy with its legs poking up and its hair hanging down, but it *had* flown. "Come on, fairy!" Deanna put her fists on her hips. "Fly down to me. I'll let you fly again, I promise. Please, fairy. Come back!" The fairy's wings fluttered a little in the breeze, as if she were trying, but nothing really happened. Deanna called to it a few more times, then sat on the ground and cried.

It was just a Barbie doll with wings she and Daddy had made. It wasn't real. Daddy was right. Fairies couldn't be real. "But I *want* a real fairy!" she wailed and flopped backward into the grass. "I *need* one!"

"What's the matter, powder puff?"

Deanna sat up and knuckled the tears from her eyes, wondering who had spoken. She looked over her shoulder at the swing. No one was there. She looked at the sandbox and the slide. Both were empty. She looked at both big gates in the high fence and they were as tightly closed as always. No one sat at the patio table. Still, someone had spoken to her and it would be rude not to answer. "My fairy won't come back."

"Oh. Maybe she likes it up here."

"Up where?"

"Up here. In the tree."

Deanna stood and peered into the leaves overhead, seeing a flash of purple and a glisten of silver as a pair of wings fluttered and . . . something—someone?— dropped down out of the leaves to a lower branch. There sat a tiny lady with short purple curls, a bright purple dress and shimmery silver wings. The little lady swung her legs, crossed at the ankles, and held on with both hands to the twig above her. She had bare feet, and toenails painted purple to match her hair. She was much prettier than the Barbie-fairy who now sat upright beside the little lady. The Barbie's feet didn't swing.

"It's nice up here. Fly up and join us."

Deanna laughed and flapped her arms. "I can't fly!"

"Really? I can."

"Are you a fairy? Will you show me how you fly?"

"I'm not a fairy, I'm an elf, and I can't do anything more until you say the magic words."

"Please," Deanna said. The elf just sat there, smiling and swinging her feet. Deanna said, "Thank you?" and the little figure still didn't move. "Hey! I said please. *And* thank you."

"Those aren't the right magic words. There are others. More special ones you have to say when you want your elf to come to you."

"What are they?"

"That depends on which elf you want to fly. You have to call her by name."

Deanna frowned. "Like Rumplestiltskin?" That wasn't a very nice name for an elf. Rumplestiltskin was ugly and her elf was beautiful.

The elf laughed and it sounded like bells ringing. "Tinkerbell!" Deanna jumped up and down, clapping her hands. She and Daddy had watched a video about Tinkerbell and a boy who could fly and a really mean guy named Captain Hook who'd scared her and made her cry.

"Nope. Close, but no cigar. If you wanted, say, for *me* to fly down and play with you, you'd have to say, 'Elf of the Morning Mist, come to me.'"

"And then you would?"

"And then I would."

"Are you really an elf? Like the kind that works in Santa's workshop at the north pole?"

The elf shook her head and wrinkled her nose as if something smelled bad. "They're distant cousins. A rowdy bunch, if you must know, and Santa lets them into the brandy much too often. That's why they have such red noses and ears. But I'm a personal elf. That means I belong to someone."

"Who?"

"You, if you want me. You wished for me, didn't you?"

Deanna nodded uncertainly. "I said I wished I had a fairy."

"Sorry, the Mother of All is fresh out of fairies today. She sent me. Elves and fairies are pretty much the same thing, you know, same powers, same mandates, but—" she blew on her fingers and brushed them on her tummy "—elves are just a whole lot more fun. Fairies can be a touch on the . . . prissy side."

"Oh."

The elf said nothing more for a minute, then spoke a bit impatiently, "Well, are you going to say the magic words or not? If you don't want me, I'm sure there are lots of little girls who do, and I don't want to keep them waiting."

"I can't remember what to say."

"Elf of the Morning Mist, come to me."

Quickly, Deanna repeated the words. The wings shimmered, purple toenails twinkled, and there stood the elf on the tall flowers by the gate. They hardly moved, sort of like when a butterfly landed on them. The elf sat down, and Deanna almost couldn't see her because her dress and hair nearly matched the flowers, like the red sock she'd lost the other day because it was lying right on top of her red skirt.

Stepping closer, she held out her hand and the elf flew onto it. Those tiny feet felt soft and warm on her palm. The elf wiggled her toes. It tickled. Deanna giggled. The elf smiled and Deanna could see she was a real person with teeth and eyelashes and everything. A real *little* person. It felt funny, being bigger than someone else. As long as she could remember, she'd always been the smallest person she knew.

Pulling her hand in closer, she took a good look at the elf, who turned around and fluttered her wings, tickling Deanna's nose and making her sneeze.

The elf turned back. "Gesundheit."

Deanna blinked and held her a bit farther away. "What does that mean?"

The elf flew off and perched on top of the slide for a minute before swooping down to the ground, saying, "Whee!" At the bottom, she didn't quite touch, but fluttered. "Gesundheit means the same as 'God bless you,'" she explained, coming back to Deanna. "Would you rather I say 'God bless' when you sneeze?"

"You mean I get to pick?"

"Sure. I'm *your* elf. You can call me Misty."

"You mean," Deanna said slowly, "you're my very own elf? Like a fairy?" Doubt and worry clouded her initial delight. "Daddy said I'd have to have a nanny instead. He said fairies aren't real."

"Hah! Have I got news for him! I'm real, powder puff. A for-sure, honest-to-goodness elf." She flew up and perched on Deanna's shoulder. "Go ahead, touch me. You'll see."

Deanna touched those warm little feet. They felt real to her. She stroked a fingertip along the bottom of one.

The elf jerked her foot away and giggled. So did Deanna.

"But still, if your daddy's going to insist on a nanny, then I'll see what I can do."

There was a shimmer of wings, a little popping sound, and there stood a lady not as big as Daddy, but lots bigger than Deanna, and a whole lot bigger than the elf. She didn't have purple hair, but sort of brown hair, and her shoes were brown, too. Her dress was green with a round white collar and she carried a brown straw purse over her shoulder on a long strap. It had a big, white button on the front.

Deanna backed up a step. "Who are you?"

The lady smiled. "I told you. I'm Elf of the Morning Mist."

"No." Deanna backed up some more. "*She* has purple hair and no shoes. And wings."

"Oh." For just an instant, the lady's hair turned purple and her shoes disappeared. Deanna jumped back right into the sandbox where she tripped on a truck and sat down hard on her bottom. Chin wobbling, she stared up at the lady.

"Are you going to cry again, powder puff?"

Deanna wasn't sure she liked the lady now. "Where did my elf go?"

The lady ran her hands down her front. "I'm right here. You said you needed a nanny. Goodness, can't you make up your mind? Really now, which would you rather have?"

"An elf. Or a fairy. But Daddy says I need a nanny. I don't know if he'd let me keep a elf. He said I couldn't have a puppy."

"An elf and a fairy are one and the same in this case, kid, but you're right. Your dad probably won't accept

an elf right off. Some guys are hard sells. That's why
I'm dressed like this. I've read the books. I've seen the
movies. I can talk the talk, even if I'm not so hot at
walking the walk. So, what do we do now? I'm new at
this nanny business.''

Deanna thought the lady must be teasing, kind of like
Daddy's friend Uncle Mark, who said lots of stuff she
didn't understand, but always smiled at her as if he liked
her a lot, so she liked him back. "You want me to tell
you what to do?''

"Sure. Like I said, I'm your elf.'' Deanna could see
now that the lady really was the elf, only with different
hair and clothes, and bigger. That was *really* magic!

"If you're my elf, does that mean you gotta do
whatever I say?''

The lady laughed, and it sounded just like bells again.
"Well, maybe not absolutely everything you say, but
most of it. I mean, if you asked me if you could stay up
all night long, I'd have to say no because it's not good
for little girls to stay up all night. Or if you asked me if
you could have chocolate cake for breakfast every day,
I wouldn't say yes.''

Deanna studied her for several minutes. "What about
just sometimes?''

The lady nodded and sat cross-legged on the grass,
tucking her dress between her knees. "If your daddy
said it was okay, too.''

Deanna knew that was unlikely and said, "Oh.''

The elf lady tilted her head to one side. Her hair
shone. A yellow-and-black butterfly sat on one of her
ears for a minute, then left. "Maybe, once in a very
long while, say if it was your birthday or something, he
might let you eat chocolate cake for breakfast.''

"What's a birthday?''

The elf's eyebrows got really high and pointed on top. "That's when you get to be one year older. You have a party with your friends, and get toys and things as presents. Sort of like Christmas, but just for you." Her eyebrows came down as she looked into Deanna's eyes. "You do know about Christmas, don't you?" Before Deanna could answer, she snapped her fingers and smiled. "Oh, of course you do. You knew about the elves in the workshop."

"When I lived at the farm, Lonnie told me all about Santa and the elves in the barn when he was milking Gertrude. He gave me a red-and-white whistle that looked like a bird, and told me about how they make toys and stuff. Grandpa took the whistle away." Remembering, she kicked at the sand and uncovered half an Oreo. It was too sandy to eat. "My grandma and grandpa don't believe in toys, and I don't got any friends."

Again, the elf's head tilted to one side. The breeze caught in her brown hair and for a minute it looked purple again. "Sure you do," she said. "You've got me and I believe in toys. And in birthday parties," she said. "Your daddy does, too."

"How do you know that? Do you know my daddy?"

"Not yet, but I will. Come on." The lady jumped to her feet, shook her dress and held out her hand. "I think it's time you introduced me to him."

Deanna took the lady's hand. It was warm and soft and felt nice. She smelled nice, too, different from Grandma Jan, different from Daddy, but nice in her own way, sort of like the purple flowers that grew tall by the gate. "What are those flowers called?"

The lady looked where Deanna pointed. "Phlox," she said. "Do you—" She broke off speaking as Daddy came outside, a big frown on his face, his mouth turned down and his legs taking very long steps. His feet were noisy even on the grass.

"Who the hell are you, and how did you get in here?" he asked, sounding very, very rude. "Get away from my daughter."

Deanna hung on with both hands as the lady tried to obey. "No, Daddy!" she cried. "Don't be mad at her. She's my—" She bit her lip and looked up at the lady who had been an elf before with wings and purple hair and a purple dress and purple eyes, and saw just an ordinary lady with brown hair and brown shoes and a green dress. Her eyes were still purple, though. "She's my very own elf. I mean, my...my *nanny*."

She knew it wasn't nice to tell lies, but maybe the elf really could be her nanny.

"Oh." Daddy looked a little less mad. "I didn't hear the doorbell ring."

The lady smiled. "I don't think anyone did."

"So how did you get in?"

The lady glanced at the gate, which stood open for the first time since Deanna had seen it, though it hadn't been open a few minutes before. "The number's on the outside of the gate."

Daddy frowned at the shiny gold numbers as if he'd never seen them before. "So I see. But there's certainly no doorbell there. What prompted you to abandon the front entrance and come around to the side?" he asked, coming to a stop right in front of the lady and looking at her still all frowny with his thumbs in his belt loops and his chin big. "Surely it would have been more professional to ring again, rather than break into an obviously private backyard."

"I heard a little girl crying, *all alone,* and thought exigency should take precedence over propriety."

Deanna blinked at the big words, and at the tone of voice the lady used. Daddy seemed to understand whatever it was she'd said, though, because he sighed really loud and then nodded. "I guess so." He looked the way Deanna had felt when he caught her with macaroni all over the floor.

2

ALAN STARED at the side gate, which had been opened only once in the time he'd lived there. He'd opened it himself, with some difficulty, to admit the men who delivered the swing-set and sandbox. Even before Deanna, he'd valued his privacy. It had always been latched from the inside with a stiff bolt. What remained to discover was how the woman, easily a foot shorter than he was, had reached over the top of an eight-foot-high gate and pushed that bolt back. Clearly, she was resourceful, which was one of the criteria he'd stipulated in a nanny.

"The agency sent you?" He shoved a hand into his hair, then wished he hadn't, then wished he hadn't wished that, and wished, too, that he'd remembered to shave that morning. "But I asked for someone older and—" He shook his head.

She made things much worse by smiling again, a totally captivating smile that did odd things to his ability to draw breath. His heart pounded. His knees weakened. It was as if he were fourteen again and looking into Kimberley Laketon's bedroom window and catching her taking her shirt off. His first sight of a girl's breasts had made him react in exactly this way. At fourteen, it might have been appropriate. At thirty-eight, it most definitely was not.

"I'm much more mature than I look," she said.

Maybe so, he wanted to say. *But suddenly, I don't think* I'm *nearly as mature as I thought I was.*

He shook his head. "No. I'm sorry, but—" He shook his head again. "It just won't do."

She smiled a sweet, quiet little smile that didn't quite make him feel she was laughing at him, but came awfully close. "You mean *I* just won't do."

"I..." He scowled, then lifted his chin. "Ah, yes. I guess that is what I mean. I mean, the nanny will need to sleep, er, *live* in and..."

She laughed. It was that which had cut through his concentration five minutes before, and hearing it again had the same effect on him. As it bubbled forth, he could hear nothing else, think of nothing else. Listening to it was like breathing delicate, luscious perfume, like biting into the most delectable dessert ever concocted and hearing the most exquisite symphony all at once, while couched on a bed of softest down. Or maybe a flying carpet.

"And you fear for your virtue," she said through her laughter.

"My...virtue?" He stared at her, feeling incredibly stupid, and awkward, and oafish. To say nothing of unshaven.

"I understand." She crossed her heart. "I promise not to molest you."

He didn't know whether to laugh aloud, or roust her out. He took refuge in a mild huff. "My virtue is not the issue here!"

His pique deepened her smile. "No? And what is? I certainly don't fear for mine. You look like a nice, harmless man who'd never do anything untoward. I'm sure no reputable agency would send a prospective nanny to you if they hadn't checked you out quite thoroughly. Besides, as a famous writer, you have a public reputation to uphold, don't you? It wouldn't look at all well in the yellow press if Alan Magnus were charged with unsavory crimes, now, would it?''

Yellow press? Unsavory crimes? She did have an odd turn of phrase. "I...well..." He stared at the ground. Dammit, it wasn't like him to mutter and fumble for words. For a moment, he watched a dragonfly whip and dart around his bare legs and feet, its wings humming audibly as it wove a pattern that struck him as being more than random. He found himself fascinated, wanting to concentrate on that rather than the matter at hand.

He forced his gaze back at the woman, struggling to say something sensible.

Words were his business, for Pete's sake. They were his livelihood. "How did you know my name?" he asked, sounding querulous, which was not at all what he'd intended. "And who told you what I—"

He shut up. Obviously the agency had told her to go to the home of Alan Magnus, and just as obviously she'd said, "Alan Magnus the writer?" and while he'd asked them not to volunteer the information, he hadn't asked them to lie for him. What he had asked—insisted, the last time he called them—was that they find him someone mature.

"I'm sorry," he said again, this time with great finality. "It's just not feasible."

"Very well," she said, turning away toward the open gate, still holding Deanna by the hand. "Come, Deanna. It's time for us to leave."

He lunged and slammed the gate shut, leaning on it while he gaped at her. "What the hell do you think you're doing? My daughter's going nowhere with you. And I told you to let go of her."

"I can't," the woman said pleasantly. "She has to let go of me. You see, I belong to her, and she's the only one who can turn me loose."

"What?" He snorted. "How could you possibly belong to my daughter?"

"She needed me, she called and I came. I've accepted the assignment. There's nothing you can do to change that."

"Watch me." She did, while he continued to stand there feeling impotent and confused. Alan tried to figure out what to do. He supposed he should call the cops to get rid of her, but his feet seemed incapable of moving from where they were planted on the grass. He had a weird vision of that hovering dragonfly having stitched him to the fabric of the earth.

She blinked her eyes. They were, he saw, purple. He'd never seen purple eyes before. And her lashes had to be false. "Well?" she asked after what seemed like a very long silence. "Are you going to do tricks?"

"*What?*"

"You said I should watch you."

Cripes! The woman was clearly a nut case. Jeez! Couldn't the agency screen its applicants better than this? "Dee," he said gently, "come here, honey. Let the lady's hand go, and come to me."

Stubbornly, Deanna clung to the woman. "But she's my *elf,* Daddy. My very own special elf."

"Your what?" It was so close to a bellow that the woman and Deanna both winced.

Deanna's small chin jutted with a stubbornness he'd never before noticed in her. "My elf."

"Did you tell her that?" Alan demanded of the woman.

"I told her my name," she said.

"Which, I suppose, just happens to be Elf?" He made no attempt to curb his sarcasm.

"Why, yes." She smiled as if he were a particularly clever puppy who'd managed to piddle on his newspaper instead of the carpet. His spine stiffened as he squared his shoulders. No half-pint woman with purple eyes was going to get the better of him.

"Elf what?"

"Elf of the Morning Mist."

He couldn't help it. He laughed. "Do you honestly expect me to believe that?"

"Certainly. Elves never lie."

"Your parents were hippies, I suppose?"

"Excuse me?"

"Who named you Elf of the Morning Mist?"

Those ridiculously long and thick dark lashes fluttered. "The Mother of All." Her tone was entirely matter-of-fact. "She names all the elves and fairies and pixies and what-have-you, though she does let Patrick name the leprechauns the odd time when a new one is created. He was *very* insistent, I'm told. Gaining sainthood went to his head, but—"

"That's enough!" Alan interrupted without compunction. How much of this twaddle did she expect him to listen to? "You were telling me about you, not about Saint Patrick and the leprechauns. Go on."

"Very well. I come from a long line of Morning Mists. There have been five thousand and twenty-two before me, but naturally, I'm the only one in existence now. The Mother of All didn't need me until quite recently."

Alan shook his head so hard he was sure his ears would fall off. He couldn't be hearing things right. *The Mother of All?* So this kook came from some kind of feminist commune. He'd heard of one over on Vancouver Island, near Ladysmith, but he thought it had disbanded a couple of years ago. Maybe this Elf of the Morning Mist was a reject from there. Or the funny farm.

"Okay," he said. "Fair enough. You can call yourself anything you want, I guess, but what name were you born with?"

"I wasn't born. I was brought into being by the Mother of All when she needed a new Elf of the Morning Mist."

As a storyteller, he could admire another expert when he heard one. If nothing else, she was as entertaining as she was good to look at. Another plus was that, for once, Deanna wasn't peppering him with unanswerable questions. She continued to stand with her adoring gaze trained on the woman as if mesmerized.

He couldn't help asking, "What happened to the prior Elves of the Morning Mist?"

Her eyes got as huge as pansies. "All of them? Oh, I'd have to read the Thousand Golden Scrolls for that answer, and 'thousand' is a misnomer. There are several thousand. Perhaps more. Or I could ask the Mother, but either way it would take years to tell you what became of each one, and quite frankly, I've never aspired to the ways of Scheherazade. Especially if it would mean spending more time on this task than strictly necessary. I see this as a quick in-and-out job. The late twentieth century is not my favorite period. Rush, rush, rush, everyone wearing timepieces, carrying telephones in their pockets. Terrible. But...oh, yes.

I was telling you about the Golden Scrolls. They go right back to the Dawn of Life, so of course I can't discuss them all. However, the Elf of the Morning Mist just before me decided to do a term as a mortal.''

She wrinkled her nose, and Alan nearly smiled. The dusting of golden freckles there did give her an elfin appearance, enhanced by her brown hair, cut short and wispy in the front to feather around the shape of her face, caressing her forehead and cheeks, but longer in back, tapering down her neck like a soft mane. And...good Lord! Were her ears pointed? He couldn't quite see. If the breeze would only lift that lock again, right there on the left, the top of her ear would be visible and—

He jerked himself back to the subject at hand. "And why would she want to become a mortal?"

"She fell in love with a mortal man." She didn't quite add *poor thing,* but he somehow sensed that was the way she felt.

"Of course," he said. "And falling in love with a mortal would naturally make her become one herself?"

"Yes, if she chose that path." Her lashes flicked way up, then down, then steadied at midpoint. His heartbeat did not.

"She could have deked out of the assignment anytime before the bug bit her. I mean, there *are* warnings, but she decided she *wanted* the whole ball of wax—marriage, house, picket fence and kids. To have that, with him, because he was a disbelieving man, she had to give up her immortality, her magic, everything that makes an elf an elf." She shook her head sadly, then shrugged.

"It was her choice, of course, but personally, I think it was a mistake. I'll never accept a term as a mortal."

"I see. A term as a mortal." He ran his tongue over his front teeth inside his lips. "Induced by the biting of a bug. Sounds like a serious virus for an...elf. How long would this, er, term be?"

"That depends on many factors. Once you're mortal, you're as vulnerable to fate as any other human being." Her answer struck him as deliberately vague. And no wonder. There was no way she could have made up this story in advance, no way to anticipate every possible question she might be asked. She was bound to come up empty once in a while.

She was also likely asked very few questions. He didn't suppose she told this wild tale to everyone she met. Only those she was trying to impress. Like little children. Or other lunatics on her ward.

"Did you tell the agency people about the Mother of All and the elves and pixies and what-have-you?"

"No. I only told you because you asked. We're not really supposed to reveal our true identities to adult mortals. Unless they ask. But if they do, we must be truthful."

"Really." He snorted. "Honey, if you think I believe one word of what you've said, think again. And if you think telling lies in front of a child is the way to impress her father into giving you the job of caring for her, reconsider that one, too."

Her purple eyes grew big and wounded looking. "I told you. I'm not telling lies. I'm incapable of it."

He gulped. Something about those eyes insisted that even if it couldn't possibly be true, *she* believed it. The thing to do, it seemed, was keep her talking until Dee got tired of holding her hand, then he'd jump her, wrestle her to the ground and hold her until the men in white coats came. He cast a speculative glance over her, wondering why, even in that shapeless, unflattering dress, she looked as if she'd be fun to wrestle with, and hold—and not for men in white coats.

He wondered if her Mother of All could spread viruses among mortal men.

Then he told himself not to be more of an idiot than he could help. It was just that, since Dee had come into his life, he'd quit dating entirely, and he was, after all, a normal, adult male with all the normal, adult male requirements, a notable one of which had not been met in some time. Not, he reflected, that Dee's arrival was solely responsible for that. He'd been too busy for a long time building a career and a reputation as a writer. Besides, writing was by necessity a solitary profession. He had no time for a social life.

He cleared his throat, wondering why he found it necessary, all at once, to justify himself to himself. Time to get his thoughts back on her, and her reason for being there. "Well, I must say that if nothing else, you have a great imagination."

She smiled cheerfully. "That would be an asset in a nanny, wouldn't it?"

"I . . . suppose so." He glanced at his daughter's rapt face. She still gazed at the woman as if she'd been shown the gates of heaven. He'd never seen Deanna look so entranced by anything. Or anyone. Himself included. Her fascination with the woman irked him.

Elf of the Morning Mist—*hah!*

Suddenly, the cleverness of her approach struck him. It was as if she'd known Deanna's aversion to the others the agency had sent, though there was no way she could have. He'd never admitted to a soul that it wasn't he who had to choose, but his daughter. He'd simply told the agency he and the other candidates hadn't quite clicked, when it was in fact Deanna's reaction and response that had warned him not to hire the earlier applicants.

Who in their right mind would let a four-year-old make that kind of decision?

He heaved a sigh. Maybe he wasn't in his right mind.

"All right, *Misty*," he said, grinning at her, wondering if she'd smile back, share the joke, one adult to another, over the head of a child. Of *course* the agency wouldn't have sent him a psychotic. They'd have been able to detect a genuine wacko right off the bat.

"Your zany story has grabbed my attention, if nothing else, and has certainly captivated my daughter, which I suppose is exactly what you had in mind. Shall we continue this interview indoors or are you happy out here?" He waved toward the patio table and chairs near the back porch. "Have a seat if you like."

She continued to meet his gaze squarely but solemnly as she, still linked with Deanna, backed up and sat on one of the chairs by the round table. "This is an interview?"

He sighed and seated himself opposite her. "Lord help me, I must be deranged, but yes. Because, like it or not, you're the only one the agency's sent around that Deanna has taken a liking to. Misty what?"

She looked startled, possibly confused, and for the first time seemed not to have a ready answer—not even a vague one.

"What's your last name," he said impatiently, "and don't give me any of that 'Morning Mist' crap, because I don't believe a word of it. I'll have name, rank and number, and everything else before this interview's concluded." He realized the agency would have all the pertinent data, but he thought a little no-nonsense brusqueness on his part would move their relationship in the direction he felt it should go, and stay—completely professional, from start to finish. She would be Miss Whatever. He would be Mr. Magnus.

With a grandmotherly nanny it might not have been so important. But with this one, and who knows what viruses might be floating around...

"Last name, please."

"Elves don't have last names, Alan," she said kindly, as if explaining something obvious to an imbecile. *Alan*... She'd called him Alan, and damned if he didn't like the way his name sounded on her lips. Maybe "Miss so-and-so" and "Mr. Magnus" would be a bit too formal under the circumstances. Maybe he could forget she needed a last name and just sing Misty—

He sighed explosively. "Dammit, woman, I told you I didn't want to hear any more of that elf stuff. Now, since my daughter seems to like you, let's get down to business. What is your last name?"

Her gaze darted this way and that before coming to rest on the blossoms by the gate as she muttered a word.

"Phlox?" he echoed with such disbelief that a flicker of hurt stained those flower-colored eyes. But dammit, she'd given herself away completely by looking at them as she swiped their name out of thin air.

"Not Phlox, *Fawkes*," she corrected him as she gently brushed a butterfly away from her ear. "Misty Fawkes." She spelled it. "At your service, sir. Or—" she smiled at Deanna, who leaned against her knee "—maybe I should say at your daughter's service, sir." She stroked Dee's hair. "For it is she who needs me." Her lashes flickered up and she met his gaze with one so candid and so deep he felt almost as if he'd been struck, then added softly, ''Most.''

Most? He sat taller in his chair, ready to let fly, glaring at her. Exactly what the hell had that meant? *He* didn't need her. Except as a nanny for his daughter.

Before he could ask, Deanna danced around the table to him, her face alight as she scrambled up on his lap and hugged him. ''Please, Daddy? Please? Can we keep her? She used to be little just like my Barbie, and sat in the apple tree swinging her feet, and her hair was purple and so was her dress and she had silver wings. Then she flew down and sat on the flowers and stood on my hand and played on the slide, and we talked and I told her I needed a nanny and she became a real, live lady. I like her, Daddy. Please don't make her go away.''

He turned Deanna and sat her on the edge of the table, where she looked like a little elf herself. ''Honey,'' he said, ''imagination is a wonderful thing to have, and I'm glad you inherited yours from me. You may go far with it, but you also have to recognize what's real, and what's pretend. I see you were pretending your Barbie could fly.'' He pointed up at the tree where the doll sat.

Deanna nodded uncertainly. ''Yes. The Barbie-fairy flew into the tree, but the real elf flew down.''

''There are no real elves,'' he said with what patience he could muster. Dammit, this woman, as much as Deanna apparently liked her, would either have to come clean, or leave. ''I know you wanted a real fairy,'' he went on, ''but remember, no matter what you and Miss Fawkes might have been pretending before I came outside, fairies aren't real.''

''But Misty is real,'' she said with deadly four-year-old logic. ''Go on, touch her. You'll see.'' She jumped down and returned to Misty's side. The woman grinned at her, then at him, and he detected something that looked very much like a challenge in her expression before her grin faded to a half-smile. She waited patiently as if she knew the outcome of the discussion in advance, but was willing to let him arrive at the inevitable conclusion in his own way, in his own time.

Drawn, despite himself, Alan leaned across the table toward her. His right hand lifted seemingly of its own volition, and his index finger curled to run down the curve of her cheek. She felt real. She felt warm. She felt smooth and soft and wholly feminine and he suddenly felt totally male, as well as completely aroused, which scared the bejesus out of him and made him snatch his hand back at the same instant as she jerked her head away.

"Mother, *no!*" Misty gasped in response to the electric charge Alan Magnus's stroking hand sent jolting through her. "That is *not* what this mission is about!"

"Excuse me?"

Appalled, Misty realized she'd spoken aloud. "Er, nothing," she said, feeling the tingle begin to recede. It might not have been the Mother, after all, and she felt like a fool for her inadvertent squawk. She and the Mother of All had had a full discussion prior to her arrival here. They had agreed that Deanna's father needed someone in his life just as much as the girl, but Misty's purpose was to help him, guide him, in finding that someone for both of them, not to become personally involved.

Certainly she might bond with the child to the point where leaving was a terrible wrench. For her. She'd done that many, many times before, and with adults, as well, especially when the need was this great. But she always eased herself out of the situation when the proper replacement came along, so as not to let the mortal feel the pain of parting. From then onward, she made only periodic clandestine visits to reassure herself that her former charges were well and happy. They never knew she was checking.

The Mother knew all that, and knew this time was no different. At least in that aspect. It was different enough that someone, the Mother, through one of the guardians had just whispered a "last" name in her ear when Alan had demanded she give one. She'd welcomed the assistance in what was an emergency, since she'd truly had no last name until just moments ago, and had been unable to lie about it. She would not welcome any further interference.

She narrowed her eyes and glared at a persistent dragonfly that seemed much too interested in these negotiations. If the Mother of All meant to play her fast and loose on this one, she'd raise such a ruckus the entire Upper World would hear it. The elves were autonomous now, whether the Mother liked it or not. And she did not. The Mother wanted everyone to take terms of mortality every couple of centuries, to relearn what the "real" world was all about. It was supposed to breed humility or something.

But in Misty's case, it would be "learn" not "relearn" because so far she had resisted all the Mother's importuning. She no more believed in humility than little Deanna's grandparents had believed in parties and fun and toys—or than Alan Magnus believed in fairies and elves. But she *was* an elf, regardless of what he wanted to believe, and she liked it that way. She also had utterly no intention of giving it up. Not for anyone. And certainly not for lust or carnal love or even romance, whatever the Mother might want for her. For her, that was not "reality." For her, reality was the freedom to come and go as the breezes blew her, like the dragonfly that had now flitted out of sight among the apple leaves, as if ashamed of having been caught eavesdropping.

Or tampering.

To her relief, when she next spoke, her tone remained quite level. "Lonely children often create imaginary friends, Alan. Surely you know that." She folded her hands, nannylike, before her on the table. "After all, isn't that the way your own very lucrative imagination got started?"

"I wasn't a lonely child." He sounded offended, but Misty didn't let that stop her fixing her gaze square on his eyes.

"Yes, you were, Alan. Your father's army career, all those moves, remember? You found your friends in books."

His mild offense teetered on the verge of out-and-out temper, and swift denial leapt into his eyes. She forestalled it by saying crisply, "At any rate, I'd recommend not enforcing your particular version of reality on your daughter." She hoped, too, if the dragonfly still hovered out of sight but within earshot, the message would also reach the ears of the Mother.

"Besides," she added, "has the agency sent anyone else remotely suitable?"

His thick brows drew together under a tumble of erotically curly black hair. *Erotically?* Hold on, Misty! What's so erotic about curly hair? Nothing, that's what.

She pulled herself back together and squared her shoulders. Alan Magnus wasn't the first good-looking mortal man she'd had dealings with and surely wouldn't be the last. Not in *this* lifetime, which she meant to see lasted well into infinity. There would be no Elf of the Morning Mist number five thousand twenty-four at all, ever, if she had her way.

"No, they haven't," he said with obvious reluctance. "But—" He clamped his lips shut and shook his head, making those untidy curls bounce on his forehead. "But what makes you so sure *you're* even remotely suitable?" He looked as if he should really be asking why *he* was considering her remotely suitable. As she knew he was.

"Deanna likes me." She made her eyes wide and innocent. "Surely that counts for something?"

He rubbed his raspy chin with the same finger he'd curved along her cheek and that intensely disturbing sensation flittered over her again. Maybe she was ailing. She knew elves weren't impervious to every malady of man.

"I guess it counts for a lot, but so does experience. How old are you?"

"Six hundred and twenty-nine."

He gaped at her for a moment, then laughed. "Twenty-nine, hmm? Okay, I guess you could be, though you don't look it. And sometimes I feel six hundred and thirty-eight, so I'll forgive you the exaggeration.

"All right," he said. "We can give it a try." He stood abruptly as if, the decision having been made, he could now escape. Striding to the apple tree, he plucked down the doll, then whirled and looked at Misty. "When can you start?"

"Start?" she repeated. "Oh, didn't you understand? I started half an hour ago."

3

"YEAH," HE SAID, frowning for a moment during which Misty thought he was trying to decide if he was making the right decision. She could have found out easily enough, but as a rule, she tried to avoid poking into other minds. When it was necessary, she did it without compunction. But doing it when it was not, purely to satisfy her own curiosity, was nothing short of snooping.

"Yes. I guess you did." He handed Deanna the doll. "Did the agency explain your duties and hours and everything?"

"I'm sure you can explain your and Deanna's needs more fully than any agency employee," she said. "But you can do that later. No doubt we'll muddle through in the meantime, won't we, Deanna?"

Deanna beamed. "You're going to stay and be my nanny?"

"I think so. Alan? Are you quite sure about this? Once I'm in, I'm in, and it won't be easy for me to leave before the job is done to my satisfaction."

In fact, it would be impossible, Misty knew. It had been impossible from the moment Deanna said the words. There were, of course, ways she could be with Deanna and help her, other than as a nanny. It was just that acting like a nanny appeared to be the best way at the moment—the best way to fulfill her entire mandate. Alan didn't need to know at this point that she had any other purpose than to care for Deanna. It would be better if he never knew it. Of course, if it became necessary, in order to gain his cooperation, she'd have to tell him.

"I . . . I'm sure," he said, after several seconds' hesitation. She heard considerable doubt in his tone, saw some reluctance in his nod, but it disappeared in the face-splitting smile he wore as he caught a cannonball of ecstatic child, hugged her tight and lifted her high.

"Is this what you really want, sweetheart?"

"Yes, Daddy. Yes! Yes! Oh, thank you!" She kissed him loudly all over his face.

When he finally set his daughter back down, Misty was ready for him, with her hand extended to clinch the deal. At the last moment, remembering the extraordinary sensation his first touch had elicited, she snatched it back and shoved it into the pocket of her dress.

Just in case her reaction to him had not been a random phenomenon or an incipient ailment.

"Maybe before you decide for certain, you should come in and see if you find your rooms suitable," he said.

"I'm sure whatever you offer me will be adequate," she said, following him up the broad steps to the back door, which hung wide open as he'd left it when he barreled through to save Deanna from her. She gazed with curiosity around the kitchen, which appeared very large to her, and full of unnecessarily complicated equipment. Luckily, she wouldn't be forced to mess with any of that.

"If you'd like, Deanna can show me where I'll sleep. That way you can get back to work and not have to bother about this anymore until after dinner's on the table.''

"Dinner? Does that mean you're willing to cook, too, without quibbling over it?"

"Of course. Food preparation is one of my specialties." She could only hope he wasn't one of those men who liked to watch a woman cooking. Clearly, Alan was not yet ready to accept her as an elf. He might find her methods of food preparation a trifle disturbing, though she was sure he'd enjoy the results just as much as if she spent all morning shopping and fifteen minutes slaving over a hot microwave.

He'd just enjoy them better, not knowing. Not yet, at any rate. When he was ready to accept her for what she really was, he'd let her know. In the meantime, though she had no intention of trying to hide anything from him, it would probably be best not to upset him unduly.

If she could manage it. She'd never been good at remembering not to do what mortals looked upon as magic things, things that came so naturally to her. She smiled and gave a quick word of thanks to the Mother of All for the powers she enjoyed.

"All right, Alan, Deanna, you've got yourselves a nanny. What would you like for dinner?"

Alan gave her a crooked grin that affected her much the same as his touch had. "Whatever you want to fix. Anything at all that I don't have to cook sounds like heaven to me. Are you sure you're not an angel?"

"Quite sure," she said. "But some of my best friends are."

"I HAD THESE ROOMS redone for a live-in housekeeper a year and a half ago." Alan's fingers feathered against the small of her back by what was likely an accident as he ushered her politely through a doorway ahead of him. The touch, as unintentional as she hoped it had been, still sent a shaft of heat through Misty's blood. Quickly, she stepped away into a cozy, cream-carpeted sitting room decorated in shades of green, with touches of bright gold and old rose as accent. All it needed was some living things. Plants, fish, birds... She'd see to that soon.

"Look, you got your own TV." Deanna swung open a cherrywood cabinet. "Can I watch it with you sometimes?"

Without waiting for a reply, Deanna danced away. "And this is where you'll sleep." Misty followed Deanna's bouncing figure through an open door into a bedroom with a walnut bureau, dressing table and nightstands—and a double bed that dominated the room in an oddly, well, *sexual* way.

Misty frowned at it. An aura filled the room, red-hot and sizzling as for a moment she saw bed covers all tangled by loving, and two warm bodies clinging together, faces obscured. She blinked and the bed stood there as neat and pristine as a showroom display. Was it a vision of past? Or of future? Not the future. Not hers. "Mother," she muttered, just in case, "you stop that right now!"

She jerked her gaze away from the bed and it collided with Alan's in the mirrored glass doors. Their mutually startled stares remained locked for a moment before he glanced away, but she knew he'd suffered from the same momentary disorientation as she had. Did *he* see visions of past and future, too, and sense auras? Some humans did, though most of those denied it even to themselves. Especially to themselves.

He swallowed and she watched his Adam's apple bob up and down. He cleared his throat and spoke briskly, his words tumbling out, fast, almost tripping over one another as if he were desperate to be done and get away from her. "I have a janitorial service in once a week now since the housekeeper quit, so you won't have to concern yourself with cleaning, but I would appreciate your cooking. There'll be extra compensation for that, of course. That's something else we can discuss later, too."

"Of course. There's no hurry."

"The bedroom has a bathroom en suite." He waved toward a closed door beyond the bed, then nodded at the mirrored doors. "And a walk-in closet."

Misty clung to Deanna's hand. "Thank you. It all looks very, um, comfortable."

It did, but moment by moment she felt distinctly more *un*comfortable. His tension and uneasiness at being even in the edge of the bedroom with her seemed to hang in the air, making it feel brittle around her, as if an earthquake were imminent. If this was the Mother's work, she was making a supreme effort to discombobulate Misty. She would not, however, succeed. Elves, unlike fairies, enjoyed total self-determination. The Mother could suggest. She could guide. But she could not force.

And she'd better quit trying. If that's what was going on here.

"And you got your own porch!" Deanna ran across the bedroom and dragged on the cord to open the drapes, flooding the room with sunlight. After wrestling briefly with the lock, Deanna cried, "Help me, Daddy."

Misty followed the others onto a wide balcony where a deeply padded chaise longue stood adjacent to a pair of white wicker chairs flanking a glass-topped table. The sight unexpectedly evoked an image of a breakfast for two laid out on the table. She envisioned a yellow rosebud in a slender vase, a steaming pot of coffee, poached eggs plump and hot on toast dripping with butter, orange wedges gleaming in the dawn light and two wicker chairs pulled out, waiting invitingly for her...and Alan.

Alan made a strangled sound beside her, muttered "What the hell?" and Misty blinked, dissolving the image.

Oh, dear! He *was* visionary. Oh, of course he was. He was a writer, wasn't he? Why hadn't she listened to him in the very beginning? He was right. This simply wouldn't do.

"Daddy's room's around there," Deanna said, gesturing toward the front of the house where the deck formed a corner and disappeared, "and mine is across the hall. I don't have a porch, but I got a princess bed with a tent thing over top and curtains on the side. Come and see, Misty."

"Yes. You, um, ladies continue," Alan said. "I'll get back to work. Your first duty can be calling the agency and telling them you have the job. The number's on a pad by the phone in the kitchen. Anything you need, or can't find, please ask. If we don't have it, we'll get it. I realize you'll need some time, of course, to go and get your things. Would this evening be all right for that?"

Things? Misty nearly repeated the word aloud as she glanced at the straw bag still slung over her shoulder. Maria hadn't left the convent in *The Sound of Music* with anything much larger than this, so surely— She brought herself up short, allowing herself a quick glance through the mirrors covering the closet, to the long hanging rods, empty of all but padded hangers, and the many shelves and drawers built into one wall. She'd need to put enough clothing in there to make it look good in case the cleaning service people snooped.

"Of course," she murmured. "That will be fine." He'd edged himself out of the bedroom and back to the sitting room, but continued to stand there, gazing at her as if he didn't quite know how to make an exit. "Thank you," she said. She wished he would go. She desperately needed time away from him, time to recover her equilibrium. Briefly, she considered disappearing, but good sense told her not to push it too far. She had the job as Deanna's nanny, a perfect forum in which to discharge the tasks required before she could consider her mission accomplished. It was a job she wanted and, with uncommon passion, to keep. It seemed vitally important that she do it. And not only for Deanna. It was equally important that Deanna's daddy be looked after, set on a steady course, as well.

She waved her hand gently, and suddenly he was at the door to the hallway. For a moment he looked nonplussed, as if he couldn't quite figure out how he'd gotten there—which of course he couldn't, or wouldn't. But instead of leaving as she'd hoped he'd do once in motion, he continued to hesitate in the doorway, his gaze still resting on her face. She tried hard not to like, quite so strongly, his blue-gray eyes, the same brooding shade as Lake Titicaca with an approaching storm in the air.

"You can park your car on the right-hand side of the garage," he said. "I'll give you a remote control for the doors. Oh, and house keys. Remind me later."

"I don't have a car."

He stared. "You don't? Oh. Then I'll drive you to where you've been living, so you can collect your belongings. But you'll really need wheels out here. Public transit's not the greatest, as I'm sure you know if you bused it today. I'll take you right after dinner."

"No, no!" The thought of being closed up in a car with Alan Magnus alarmed her. "There's no need for you to put yourself out. Truly. I'll be fine. And I don't need a car."

"Trust me," he said. "You'll need a car. I don't mean you have to buy one of your own. There are two here. You and Deanna can use the station wagon. It was my sister's, but she left it for me to look after when she took a position with Doctors Without Borders. The pretense is that she might want it again someday, but we both know better. She's more at home in a Land Rover on some African veld than driving a station wagon around town." He shrugged.

Leaning against the doorjamb, he looked cool and elegant and extremely masculine in his white shorts and peach-colored golf shirt. "I've never driven it, but I have started it once in a while to keep its battery up. After I get it serviced, it's yours."

Misty frowned. "I don't know how to drive a car."

He stared and shouldered himself erect. "What? Why not?"

It really would be best if he didn't ask questions like that, questions she couldn't answer indirectly or evasively. "Because elves don't need cars. I fly everywhere I want to go."

He lowered his lashes till they nearly covered his eyes. His expression made her wish she were able to lie. "Misty..." His tone held a dark warning.

"Yes, Alan?"

"You are not an elf, and you cannot fly. No more fairy tales, okay? Nothing but the truth, the whole truth and all that, unless it's just you and Dee and you're having a game of pretend. And then I want you to be sure *she* knows it's pretend."

She lifted her head. "Whatever I tell you, Alan, or Deanna, will be the truth. I told you, I'm incapable of lying, and even if I were, I would never lie to a child."

"Right." His expression said *wrong,* but she let it go. There was nothing else she could do. "You'll have to get a driver's license," he added, as if elves got driver's licenses every day.

Reluctantly, she nodded, staring down at her ugly brown shoes. From what she'd observed, automobiles must truly be a tedious means of transportation. There was no more *whee* in them than there was beauty in her shoes.

"Misty, if you've had your license taken away for any reason, I think I have a right to know, since you'll be the person responsible for my daughter's safety when I'm not with her."

She lifted her head quickly, wondering if she could back out of this assignment. But no. That was the one thing she could not do. She was here to see to Deanna's future. She had no choice but to stay. And to deal with him.

"I am a very responsible . . . person." It was difficult to so demote herself, but okay, if he didn't want her to refer to her status, she wouldn't. Besides, elves were people, in a way, just different people. "I will do no harm to Deanna, nor allow any harm to come to her as long as I am her . . . nanny."

He stared at her for a moment, an odd expression on his face. "I didn't ask you to swear an oath."

"Nevertheless, I felt you needed me to."

He sighed. "I've offended you. I'm sorry."

"Don't be. I understand. Deanna is very important to you. She's very important to me, too. I wanted you to know that."

His "I do know that—" cut across her "And so are you." He broke off, stared at her for a moment, then turned swiftly and strode away.

Deanna tugged at her hand again, demanding that they go and see *her* room.

Naturally, Misty obeyed the demand.

IT WAS HER LAUGHTER that got him. Alan ground his back teeth as the merry sound broke his concentration for the tenth time, forcing him to look out the window. She and Deanna were obviously having a wonderful time, though at the moment he couldn't see them. With a muttered curse, he dragged his focus back to the screen in front of him.

When, moments later, the excited yipping of a puppy blended with the feminine laughter, he leapt to his feet, knocking his mouse to the floor and sending his chair rolling back to crash into a bookcase.

Misty stood over Deanna's stuffed dog, the one he'd bought her after Mark had broken her heart by offering a live one he'd had to turn down on her behalf. It was a floppy thing with one brown ear, one white and covered with big brown splotches on its mostly white coat. He'd hoped she'd keep it on her bed, but there it was, bouncing across the grass, making yelping sounds.

Or rather, Misty made the yelping sounds, and she must have affixed strings to the toy somehow, because it appeared to be jumping up against first her legs, then Deanna's, then leaping high toward Misty's out-stretched palm. Deanna ran in big circles, Misty and the toy dog ran with her as if the dog were nipping at Deanna's heels. She kept looking over her shoulder, stumbling as she ran, shrieking with laughter.

Lord, that thing looked almost real in action. Misty must be a master puppeteer. And her sound effects were amazing. Might be a bit of ventriloquism there, though he'd never seen it in action before except on television. What she did with that toy pup fascinated him. Hell, he couldn't even see its strings. It seemed to dance as lithely and as easily as she did herself.

He noticed her feet were bare.

Seeing her like that, he was glad she'd shed the ugly shoes. Her feet were small and pink, a pretty, warm shade. He'd wondered if they ever got cold, and thought about warming them in his hands. As the thought crossed his mind, she whirled and looked right at him as if she could see him through the slats of the blind. Oddly, he felt guilty for having lusted after her feet and was about to slink from the window when she turned away.

When Deanna plopped down on the grass under the apple tree, the toy went limp beside her legs. For Pete's sake, it even appeared the dog's tongue was lolling! Alan squinted into the blend of sun and shade beneath the tree, but then Misty flopped down flat on her back with her arms outspread and one knee bent, hiding the toy from view.

A smile curved his mouth as he went back to work.

To his amazement, he accomplished more in the balance of the afternoon than he had in the five days previous.

It was good, knowing Dee was happy and safe and entertained. He felt better about everything now. He was right to have hired Misty.

THREE DAYS LATER, he wasn't so sure of that after one of the house-cleaning crew ended up in hysterics and Alan had to question not only his own eyes but his own sanity.

It started out as such a great day, too.

Misty had a perfect breakfast ready for him the minute he came downstairs from his postjog shower. He'd missed his morning jog since becoming a father and was glad he could get back to it again. It gave him greater pleasure to have a meal provided when he arrived home starved. He enjoyed every bite of his scrambled eggs, crisp bacon and flavorful hash browns; Misty's home-made bread made superb toast, and her incomparable coffee encouraged not just seconds, but thirds. Mostly, though, he reveled in watching the loving interaction between her and Deanna.

"Which is the best park to take Deanna to play?" she asked him as he sat over his third cup, rather than going to work.

He gave her directions, and watched the two of them out of sight before reluctantly closing the door. Before he got settled at his computer, the cleaning service arrived and set to work, leaving him free to do his own.

He'd just gotten deeply involved when a piercing scream tore through the air. Leaping up, he ran from the room. The scream came again, from upstairs.

"Harry! Harry!"

As Alan raced up the stairs two at a time, a man tore out of the kitchen, thundering after him. A woman wearing a white smock backed out of Misty's room, still yelling, her eyes round with shock. Heading blindly toward the stairs, she cannoned into Alan, who had just enough time to brace himself, and was prevented from falling by the other man smashing into his back.

Alan set the woman back upright, eyes searching for blood or protruding bones. She appeared to be intact and unhurt, but staring eyes in a gaunt face evinced real terror.

"Harry...Harry..." she gasped. "You won't believe it. You gotta see it. It's crazy. Didn't I tell you I don't like this house? It's spooky, I said, set back like that from the street with all those trees and shrubs, making it impossible to see into the grounds. It's—"

"Milly!" Harry put his hands on Milly's bony shoulders and gave her a little shake. "Calm down. What happened? What did you see?"

She looked, Alan thought, as if she'd seen several ghosts.

"Grass," the woman said. "There's grass in there." She rolled her eyes toward Misty's suite.

The man groaned and rolled his eyes toward Alan. "She's new."

Turning back to his colleague, he continued sternly, "Now you listen here, Milly. Calm down, I said. Get a grip." He gave her another little shake. "The boss briefed you this morning. Whatever you hear or see in a client's home is that client's business and no one else's. Right?"

"Yes, but—*grass*, Harry? In a *bed*room?"

He puffed out an impatient breath. "So what?" he said. "I've run into plenty of other...substances in houses I've cleaned. It's no big deal. Besides—" he gave Alan a sickly smile over his shoulder "—what's a little grass between friends?"

Alan's mind reeled. Not his perfect new nanny! Oh, no! Please! He needed her, but not if she—

Milly jerked free. "Not that kind of grass, you moron!" She gave a disgusted snort. "I mean *grass*-grass, like a lawn, where there should be a carpet. And a canopy of flowers and stuff over the bed with no visible means of support. With birds and butterflies in it. And..." She paused, glaring first at Harry, then at Alan. "And, there are rabbits eating that grass. As well as doing what rabbits do when they eat. For crying out sideways! Am I supposed to vacuum up rabbit raisins every week?"

4

"RABBIT WHAT?" Harry and Alan echoed as one. "Do you mean—"

"Yes! There's a limit, you know, to what we're expected to clean, and that room goes beyond it, I tell you. There's a waterfall, too, and the oddest little man sitting beside it playing a flute. He's *naked!*"

Harry backed up a step. "Uh, Milly—speaking of grass, have you—?"

"Dammit, no! And this is not my imagination!" She waved at the door. "Go on, have a look for yourself."

Before Harry could move, Alan strode through the door into Misty's sitting room. Everything looked normal, except for the long snake of the hose from the built-in vacuum system lying coiled on the floor. The carpet looked freshly vacuumed. With the other man crowding him from behind, he stepped over the hose into Misty's bedroom.

"Right. In there. See it?" Milly demanded from a safe distance.

Alan stepped aside to let Harry in.

"Yeah," Harry said. "I see a bed, a carpet, drapes, dressers and stuff." He picked up the cleaning supplies Milly had left on the bureau. "Nothing else, Milly. Nothing weird, and no lawn, no flowers or butterflies or birds, no bunnies." He turned and gave her a hard look. "And no naked men."

"But they were there! I saw them. I..." Milly shoved past Harry, a look of bug-eyed apprehension on her face.

"*What?*" she croaked. She swayed. Alan looked at her. Her face was still white, but now it wore a puzzled expression as she surveyed the room decorated exactly as it had been the last time Alan saw it. Its carpet, too, looked freshly vacuumed, except...

Except for what was indisputably a short trail of rabbit raisins leading under the bed.

Before he knew what he was doing, Alan put himself between the woman, Harry and the evidence, hiding it.

"I don't understand," she moaned. "It was all there, just like I said. *Really!*" She backed out of the room, but hovered in the doorway, casting yet another crazed stare around. Alan glanced down, and blinked. The rabbit raisins were gone. Suppressing a grimace, he gingerly lifted his foot in case he'd misjudged its placement. But no. There were no squashed pellets on the carpet. He breathed again. Damn! That woman had him almost believing in her hallucinations. Of course there'd been nothing on the floor, any more than there'd been a naked little man, birds, butterflies or a water-fall. Jeez! *He* needed to get a grip, too.

Harry shoved the tray of cleaning supplies at Milly and thrust her back into the sitting room. He wound up the vacuum hose as he tried to apologize. "I don't think she's cut out for this line of work, Mr. Magnus. Too emotional. Too high-strung. I told the boss. I said, Elsie, don't hire that one. She looks nervous."

He made an offended sound. "Women. They never listen. Especially not to something they don't want to hear about one of their own kind. But trust me on this one, Mr. Magnus. It won't happen again. I'll insist on bringing an experienced helper next week. One who doesn't suffer from delusions."

The coiled hose draped over his shoulder, he pushed the woman toward the stairs.

"Come on, Milly," he said wearily after stowing the hose and the cleaning supplies in a closet. "I'll drive you home before I go on to the next client. We're finished here, aren't we?"

"Finished here?" She glanced apprehensively at Alan, who had entered the kitchen behind Harry. "Finished? You're dang right we're finished here. At least, I am. For good. No, I don't care what you say, Harry," she added, though Alan had heard no argument from the other man. "Nothing will get me back in that room. Nothing will get me back in this house. I know what I saw. I know what I heard. And that little man was sitting there wearing nothing but skin, playing music while the rabbits danced."

"Milly, face it, there's two of us here as witnesses, and we don't see anything out of the ordinary."

He looked at Alan as if for confirmation. So did Milly. "Nothing," Alan said, spreading his hand. "Everything looked normal to me." It had. The rabbit raisins hadn't really been there. His imagination, triggered by Milly's wild story, had just gone into overdrive.

"But... but... you're *guys!*" she said as if that explained their inability to see what she had seen.

"Come on, Mil. You'll feel better soon." Harry steered her out the door.

As it swung shut behind them, Alan heard her continuing to protest. "He had horns, Harry! I just remembered. The little man had horns on top of his head, and his feet weren't like yours and mine. I think he was a devil. He wasn't red, but I truly believe he was a . . ."

BY THE TIME Misty and Deanna came home from the park, Alan had all but put the incident from his mind. He considered mentioning it to Misty, to laugh about it with her, but there were too many other things to hold his interest. Such as the way her skin glowed after a walk on a windy beach, the way her arm felt when he inadvertently brushed it with the back of his hand as he pulled her chair out for her when lunch was on the table.

That night, after one of her superb dinners, he thanked her and said, "Misty, there are things we need to discuss. Could I see you in my study at, say, eight-thirty?

She smiled as she stood and began gathering up dishes. "Of course, Alan. Which one?"

He blinked. "Which one what?" As far as he knew, he had only one study.

She looked momentarily puzzled in the way she had that made her sometimes seem almost otherworldly, as if she didn't fully understand his phrasing and needed to translate it to another language before it made sense. That was ridiculous, of course. She spoke perfect English.

"Which eight-thirty?" she asked. "It happens twice a day on Earth, doesn't it? I'm sorry to sound obtuse, but time, as *you* know it, doesn't exist in the Upper World, so it's best if you're precise when instructing me."

For a moment, he thought she was serious, then he laughed, realizing she was poking gentle fun at him, getting back into her elf persona. Oddly, he liked it. It made him smile. "This evening, please."

"I'll be there. Will you have coffee now, or later, or both?"

"When you come into the study will be fine. And bring two cups."

She nodded. "As you wish."

He should have gone right back to work, but didn't. He could do nothing but sit in front of his computer and try to put Misty out of his mind. He'd almost succeeded when she brought Deanna to him, all pink and warm and bathed, ready for bed.

"Well!" He smiled from Deanna's ruffly nightgown to Misty's slightly damp-around-the-edges form. Her hair made little spiky arrows on her forehead and temples, emphasizing her eyes, which needed no emphasis at all. "You two look like you've had a good time."

"Thanks. We did. Deanna tells me it's been your habit to tuck her in and read her a story. I'm sorry I haven't offered you a chance to do that before. I think she misses it."

"I'm the one who's sorry," he said, nestling his sweet-scented daughter into his arms. "I've been letting my work consume too much of my time. But that's partly your fault, Misty. You make my life so uncomplicated. I don't know what I ever did without you, and hope I never have to find out again." Holding out a hand to her, he added, "Shall we share the task?"

"I—" Whatever she'd started to say, she didn't finish, then suddenly, though he'd scarcely had time to blink, she was just...gone. If it hadn't been for the door closing softly behind her, he could have sworn she'd simply disappeared. Damn! Disappointment curled like a snake in his belly.

Until she was gone, he hadn't realized exactly how much he'd wanted her to help him tuck Deanna in, which made no sense at all. Before Misty's arrival, he'd happily tucked his daughter in without assistance. It was not a task he'd intended to give up. Or even share.

And Misty certainly deserved a bit of time to herself. Usually, by Deanna's bedtime, he was wiped out completely, so limp he could scarcely get back to his computer. Mornings always seemed to come too soon. Since she'd come, Misty had scarcely had a moment to herself. No wonder she'd brought Deanna to him this evening. It was her subtle way of telling him it was his turn.

That was another thing they'd need to discuss in addition to her wages—her time off. It had to be scheduled on a regular basis so they'd both know where they stood. There might be nights he'd want to go out now that it was possible. And surely there'd be evenings she'd like to do the same.

Oh, yeah? With whom?

The instant, instinctive question brought him up short. But hell, why shouldn't he feel that way? As long as she worked for him, he was responsible for Misty, and in many ways, she appeared very unsophisticated, innocent. She might be old enough, but the idea of her dating men did not sit well with him at all.

When he left Deanna's room, Misty's door was closed. He forced down his disappointment and went back to work, knowing he'd be seeing her at eight-thirty.

The thought was oddly uplifting.

EIGHT THIRTY-FIVE. Eight forty-eight. Eight fifty-two. For someone who'd asked *him* to be precise, she showed a distinct disregard for punctuality. Alan flung his newspaper onto the floor, heaved himself out of his favorite chair and kicked at one of the logs he'd set into the fire more than half an hour before, wanting the room to look cozy and welcoming. Sparks flew upward.

Where the hell was she? Had she forgotten? Had she fallen asleep? He frowned. What if Misty hadn't merely fallen asleep? What if she were ill? Would she call him, or would she suffer in silence?

Of course she'd call him if she were ill. She might be a tad naive about some things, but she had a good head on her shoulders or he'd never have entrusted his daughter to her. She'd simply gotten busy doing something and forgotten.

What, he wondered, lowering himself back to his chair, determined to appear relaxed and unconcerned when she did appear, did she do up there in her room after Deanna was asleep? Watch television? Read books or magazines? Knit? Crochet?

Or did she fly out the window and go visit the other fairies? Oops. *Elves.* He smiled, chuckled, then leaned his head back and laughed outright.

What an imagination she had, and how Deanna still hung on her every word. Of course, Dee wasn't sophisticated enough to know that Misty's entire story was as screwball as they come. Everyone above the age of four knew quite well elves didn't have wings. That was fairies. Misty should at least have tried to get it straight. He grinned. Elf of the Morning Mist, indeed. He much preferred to think of her as a real woman. He—

He jerked up straight in his chair. *No, he did not prefer to think of her as a woman!* He much preferred to think of her as a real *nanny*. That he thought of her as a woman at all was disturbing and irritating and about to stop. He didn't have time for a woman.

Rising again, he paced across the room, turned, paced back and stared at the mantel clock again. Two full minutes had passed. When it wheezed and bonged its Big Ben chimes, he stood counting them all the way up to nine, then set the screen before the fire and strode from his study.

First, he checked on Deanna, then gaped in disbelief at her bed with a terrible sensation of dread sinking through his insides. Empty! Gone! Nothing there but tumbled covers and that floppy stuffed dog she and Misty played with so often. Oh, God! Deanna!

He all but leapt across the hall, knocked on Misty's door, listened, received no reply and knocked again, louder.

Gnawing at his lip as fear gnawed at his gut, he tried the knob. It opened smoothly. The room was dark, with only faint illumination coming in from distant street lamps to show that it was empty. The bedroom door stood open, the bed neatly made. There was no sign of either Misty or Deanna.

"No..." he said softly. "No. Oh, no. Not like this." He clenched his fists, squeezed his eyes shut as pain racked him, loss, grief and anger. *Oh, God, I trusted her, and all along, they must have sent her.*

He hadn't really thought Pippa's parents would make good their threat to take Deanna back from him, but... oh, Lord! There had to be another explanation! *Please!*

A soft, childish laugh sliced through his thoughts and he spun toward the drapes fluttering over the French doors.

Pulling a small gap between the panels, he peered out.

Misty lay curled on the chaise longue, feet tucked beneath her, a blanket-wrapped Deanna cuddled into the curve of her body. Both leaned their heads back and stared up at the spangled sky.

"That's Cassiopeia. And see, over there is Orion. Someday I'll tell you a story about Orion and his dogs."

"Are his dogs fairy-dogs?"

Fairy-dogs? He'd have to ask one day exactly what constituted a fairy-dog. It conjured up a picture of a dog with cellophane wings. Maybe those strings Misty attached to Dee's dog turned it into a "fairy-dog." Alan grinned as Misty answered, "In a way, I guess you could say they were. Now, can you tell me which one's the Big Dipper?"

"That one," Deanna said, poking her arm out from under the blanket and pointing toward a spot just over the horizon, earning herself a murmur of congratulation. "I like the stars, Misty. Where did they come from?"

"The Mother of All sprinkles them in the night sky for us."

"Why doesn't she do it in the daytime, too?"

"Because then they wouldn't be special. Wait till she says we can make you an aurora. Oh! That *is* fun."

"What's a 'rora?"

"It's when all the elves and pixies and fairies everywhere, here on Earth, and those still in the Upper World, hold a big party. We all take fiery torches—like sparklers—and—"

"What's sparklers?"

Misty sighed and smiled, tucking Deanna's arm back under the blanket. "That's something else I'll have to show you soon."

"Okay. Then what do all the elves and fairies do with their torches?"

"We ride the waves of heaven, up and down and around, circling the earth and sun and all the moons and planets, making big, wide bands of light shimmer and shiver and sway among the stars, dancing as the angels sing. It's a beautiful sight. Some night, when I know there's going to be an aurora, I'll come in and wake you and bring you out here to see it."

"Does 'rora light fix up bad dreams the same way starlight does?"

"Oh, yes, but you won't have to have a bad dream first before you get to see it."

Deanna tilted her head farther back against Misty's arm. "Are there lots more fairies and elves and stuff, up there with the stars and the 'rora? Is that the Upper World? It's *very* upper up there where the stars are, isn't it? Even more upper than this balcony and that's even higher than Daddy's head."

Alan saw Misty smile again and drop a kiss onto Deanna's brow. "The stars are very 'upper,' little one. But the Upper World is not there. It's between here and there, between waking and sleeping, between the morning breeze and the evening tide. It's everywhere and everywhen all at the same time."

Deanna wiggled her arm out of the enfolding blanket again and reached upward. "Can you touch the stars from the Upper World, Misty?"

"Sometimes it feels like that."

"I'd like to touch a star. I'd like to hold one."

Misty laughed and sat them both upright, making a nest for Deanna between her knees. "Of course you would. Here."

Alan stared as she made a slight gesture with her fingers and a small, bright light glowed in Deanna's hand. "Hold it gently," she said. "Cup it with your other hand, too, so it doesn't slip away too fast."

Deanna laughed in delight and sat cupping the light, head bent over it. It silvered her pale, fluffy hair, illuminated her enchanted face, and slowly, slowly, it faded.

"It's gone," Dee said sadly, opening her hands.

"You can have another one some other time. Cuddle up now, and I'll tell you a story." Settling down again, she wrapped the blanket tenderly around Deanna and began.

"Wynken, Blynken and Nod, one night, sailed off in a wooden shoe..."

Several minutes later, Alan realized his mouth was still open and closed it. Wordlessly, he slipped through the drapes and took a chair nearby. Misty glanced at him as she patted his daughter gently and continued to weave her own "nets of silver and gold" about the child.

By the time the rhyming story was done, Deanna slept.

Misty and Alan continued to sit in silence, feeling the night fold softly around them. She looked at him, and slayed him with a smile.

"I was worried when you didn't come to my study at the appointed time," Alan said presently when he felt he could speak lucidly. He kept his voice low partly to prevent disturbing Deanna, partly because he was afraid it would shake.

"I'm sorry." He could see that she meant it. "I was about to leave when Deanna woke from a nightmare. I told her that the stars could cure bad dreams, and she asked me what were stars so I brought her out to show her.''

She tilted her head as she studied him. "Deanna's education has some strange gaps, Alan.''

That made him defensive. "Because she doesn't know about stars? Do most small children? What if they've never been outside at night?''

"She didn't know what a birthday was, either, until I told her.''

"What?" Her statement had sounded very much like an accusation. "Certainly she knows what a birthday is," he scoffed. "She's had three of them in her lifetime and—'' He broke off, spurt of annoyance subsiding. After all, three birthdays weren't that many, and it was hardly likely she'd remember the first two. Maybe not even the third one, if no one had made a fuss over it. He sighed. As of course no one had, not back at Pippa's parents' farm. She had one coming up, and likely didn't know that, either.

"Dee never mentioned her birthday, and I guess I haven't either. It's not till the third of October." That, he realized as he spoke, was less than three weeks away.

He gave his head a quick shake. "But it certainly never occurred to me that she might not know what one was.''

Then, speaking more to himself than to her, he added, "They have a lot to answer for, her grandparents.''

"The ones who don't believe in toys?''

He shot her a quick look. "Exactly." Had Deanna told her that, or... Of course Dee had told her that! Any other notion was patently ridiculous. Including the one that Deanna's grandparents might have somehow sent Misty to steal her away. No one would be able to fake the tenderness with which she held a child, rocked her and soothed her. This nanny was the real thing, all right, and she already loved Deanna. He and his daughter were both lucky the agency had sent her.

"Her mother and I weren't married," he said abruptly, then frowned, wondering what possessed him, telling this stranger intimate details of his life—except in the few days since she'd come, sharing meals with them, just being in their house, their lives, she had ceased to be a stranger. He realized Misty was fast becoming as important to him as she was to Deanna. Somehow, just knowing she was in the house, that he might hear her voice, her laughter, at any moment, catch a whiff of her scent, placed his normal sense of loneliness and isolation outside him, remembered but no longer a real part of him.

She said nothing, but something in her expression encouraged him to continue. He found it impossible not to.

"I can't understand why Pip stole those first years of Dee's life from me. I wasn't in love with her, nor she with me, but we had *something* together, I thought."

"Yes. A child."

Her tone was light, completely nonjudgmental, yet he felt the urge to explain further, as if it were important she know the truth. Know *him*. He wanted to answer all the questions she'd never asked.

"But we didn't have her 'together,'" he said, then explained about Pippa's unexpected departure. "I didn't learn of Deanna's existence until late February this year. Pippa's letter reached me in a roundabout way, routed here and there through two publishers' offices and my agent's, and finally arrived several months after she wrote it. Not only had I changed publishers since Pippa knew me, I had moved several times. I guess I was hard to track down.''

She made a small, encouraging sound, and he continued. ''The letter was sent on via a lawyer, who had received it from a doctor, who had initially tried to reach me though my first publisher. In it, I learned that Pippa had taken Deanna to visit her parents, and while she was there, she was badly injured in a car crash. She knew she was dying. She managed to scribble a note to me, and asked a doctor to find me, to explain in person about Deanna, and then to give me the note.

''When the publisher refused to divulge my address, and seemed to be taking their own sweet time about passing on her letter, the doctor hired a lawyer out of her own pocket.

''The lawyer convinced my publishing house it was serious business, contacted my agent, who contacted me, and then I learned I had a daughter.''

Misty smiled at him, cradling Deanna closer, resting her cheek on the child's soft hair. ''And went and got her.''

''Yes.'' He hitched himself closer and wrapped one of Dee's dainty curls around his forefinger, just brushing Misty's chin in passing. She jerked her head up. He snatched his hand back to the safety of his chair, gripping the arm so tightly the wicker creaked.

''Pippa's parents act the way the couple in the painting *American Gothic* look. They belong to some fundamentalist religious sect that eschews pleasures. Pippa loved her parents, but couldn't live with them. She left when she was legally of age to do so, and went back only for rare visits. She was a free spirit, Pippa was.''

After several silent moments had passed, Misty said, ''And now her spirit is truly free.''

"I guess."

She reached out and touched his hand with soft fingertips. "I *know*," she said with utter conviction that somehow managed to convince even a skeptic like him.

Grateful, he smiled, turned his hand over and captured her fingers. This time, neither of them broke the contact. Warmth radiated from his hand, up his arm and surrounded his heart. Their gazes met, held, and Misty blinked first, then slowly withdrew her hand, resuming patting Deanna.

"Despite all the documentation I had proving I was her father, it took until April for me to get a court order saying I could take her. The day I met Deanna was the day we left there. Her grandparents tried to stop me, but there was nothing they could do. She took to me right away."

He shook his head in remembered amazement. "It was uncanny, the immediate bond between the two of us. Almost as if we'd been waiting for each other all our lives."

Misty laughed softly, a delicate web of sound that cast itself over him. "Silly. You had been. She needed you. You needed her." She didn't say it aloud, but something suggested she had added silently, *As much as you both need me.* Again, her conviction startled him, though he dared not comment on her unspoken words because he must have imagined them.

"Maybe," he said. "At any rate, it was the happiest day of my life."

"And hers, too, I suspect."

"Oh, I don't know about that. I'm certain Pip was a good mother to her, and that they loved each other a lot. My biggest regret, apart from missing so much of her life, is that I don't even have a photograph of her to give to Deanna.''

"Her memories are there," Misty said comfortingly, "whether she can see them consciously or not. Childhood memories never quite leave. And they all leave their marks.''

"Yes, but I still wish she had a picture." He put his feet up on the end of her chaise and leaned back, his hands behind his head. "I think you gave her a couple of memories tonight she'll always cherish. Her first sight of stars, and her first firefly.''

"Firefly?"

He felt a chill as he remembered there were no fireflies along this part of the Pacific coast. "Then...what was that you gave her to hold?''

She shrugged. "Just a bit of magic." The starlight reflected in her eyes, twinkling back at him. That, too, was a bit of magic.

"I should carry Deanna back to bed for you. She gets heavy when she's sleeping.''

"She's fine. I like holding her.''

He liked sitting with his feet near Misty's, liked looking at her reclined on that gracefully crafted wicker daybed his mother had found for him at a garage sale. Misty looked exotic, sexy and old-fashioned, all in one package. Some kind of flowing gown replaced the dress she'd worn earlier. He wondered if her feet, tucked up in its folds, were bare. He suspected they were. Yes, Misty was a barefoot type by nature.

Once more, he wondered if her feet were cold, and experienced a strange need to hold them in his hands, making sure they were warm.

It was downright uncanny, the way she pulled them in closer to her body as the thought crossed his mind.

He experienced another little chill, and struggled again against the tendency to wonder if she could possibly read his mind. No, dammit. No one could read minds!

He shot to his feet. "Nevertheless, it's time Deanna was in bed. Then maybe we could have that coffee we were supposed to have earlier. We do have things to discuss."

"Of course," she said, standing.

Inadvertently, he glanced down at her feet, but the hem of the gown covered them, pooling slightly on the deck, and as she moved, it shimmered. She took one step toward him. The fabric whispered, releasing a sweet flower scent. He breathed it deep, staring at her over top of his sleeping child.

He wanted to tell her to sit back down, that he'd get the coffee, that they could share it there under the stars with the night sweet and silent and scented around them. He tried to speak, but no words came.

Instead, Misty spoke. "You'd like to have coffee out here?"

He stared at her and slid Deanna out of her arms, careful not to touch Misty more than was necessary. She *could* not know what he'd been thinking. Probably, she'd been thinking it, too. The thought disturbed him as much as the previous one, not that the idea didn't badly tempt him. But for one thing, it was too cold for her to be sitting outside in that wispy gown of hers. For another— He puffed out a quick breath. "No. In the living room, please."

Even his study was too small a room; it would be too intimate with the fire he'd lit earlier still glowing on the hearth, the stack of CDs in the player emitting moody music. He must have been out of his mind. What had he been thinking of? It wasn't as if he'd consciously been setting up a scene for seduction. Far from it.

He'd told himself he was only making the room comfortable, inviting, hoping to put Misty at her ease when she came in with the coffee. The realization there had been more to it churned his insides for a moment until he sorted it out in his mind.

It had been nothing more than a small error in judgment, not something he need upset himself over. He wasn't the first man to have put himself on the edge of an abyss, nor was he the first to pull back when he felt himself begin to teeter. Not that he really sensed danger ahead where Misty was concerned, but it might be more prudent to change his plans.

In the living room, he'd turn on all the lights and switch off the sound system. He didn't need any more enchantment, any more bits of magic. Nor any more heady scents.

"And bring that driving book with you," he said over his shoulder. "I want to see how you're doing with it."

Driving lessons. Yes. That was prosaic enough to keep him firmly rooted in reality. As he tiptoed away carrying Deanna, he realized with relief it hadn't been Misty's perfume he'd smelled, but the aroma of the phlox in the garden.

Just as soon as he got his revisions done, he'd cut the flower stalks back, as he did every autumn. They were well past their best. Time for them, and their evocative scent, to go.

5

If Alan, who was, in effect, her employer as long as she was, in effect, Deanna's nanny, hadn't expressed it as an order, she wouldn't have been there. Misty knew she was growing much too fond of Alan Magnus's company, and that he was intriguing her like no other man ever had.

That, she needed to keep foremost in her mind—he was just a man. His thought processes and emotional patterns, his natural aura, should have held no secrets from her. Yet they did. He was a difficult man to read, and so much of what she should have seen instinctively remained clouded. It was, she thought, as if a gauzy curtain lay between his psyche and hers, tantalizing by revealing, then teasing by obscuring. Always, she was compelled to look closer, to probe deeper. Each time the view cleared momentarily to reveal another fascinating glimpse of Alan Magnus, the man, she wanted very badly to maintain the moment. Then a subtle change would come over his features, making him maddeningly, frustratingly inscrutable.

As Misty carried the coffee tray into the living room, Alan jumped up to relieve her of the burden, setting it on the coffee table. The book she carried under her arm fell to the floor.

be faced with having to share the small, enclosed space with Deanna's daddy while he transported them. Yes, learning to drive herself would be safer.

She connected her mind to her mouth and gave him the right answer.

TWENTY MINUTES LATER, Alan flapped the book down on the arm of the sofa and smiled at Misty. "You're good. Very good."

She had truly impressed him. Obviously she'd studied hard. "If you can do as well in your written test tomorrow, you'll ace it and earn your learner's."

Her pansy eyes glowed for a second behind the shadowy thicket of her lashes, and a dimple he'd never noticed flickered at the corner of her mouth. "But I got one wrong." Despite her protest, he knew his praise delighted her.

"One wrong isn't bad," he said quickly to protect himself against the risk of getting lost in a minute examination of her face, the varying shades of her eyes, the shape of her chin, the texture of her skin, the gleam of her moist lips when she ran her tongue over them.

"I'm sure you won't miss it during the real test."

Her eyes narrowed. "What would happen if I did?"

"One wrong? Nothing."

"What would happen if I made a mistake driving? Would they take my license away?"

He grinned, knowing exactly where this was taking them. "Sorry, Misty. You don't get out of it that easily. They don't snatch your license unless you commit a really serious offense, like drinking and driving. For something minor, you get off with a warning."

She sighed. "Oh."

"Trust me, okay? It will work. As soon as my parents get back from vacation, they'll look after Misty and we'll start your lessons."

"*You'll* give me lessons?" Her eyes widened in horror, disbelief or relief, he couldn't be sure which. "I thought people had to go to driving school."

He considered for a second sending her to one, but rejected the notion at once. What if she told the instructor she was an elf? He'd expel her. They didn't knowingly give crazy people driver's licenses. They did it unknowingly all the time, but—what was he thinking? Misty wasn't crazy. She might have an odd delusion or two, but on the other hand, she might not. He still hadn't been able to decide if she really believed her preposterous claim, or merely used it to tease him.

Hell, everything about her teased him. And tempted him, and fascinated him—even her quirky assertions. But would an outsider feel the same way about her? It wasn't worth taking the risk. Better to teach her himself.

"Yes. I'll give you your lessons. And don't worry. I have every confidence you'll be a fine driver."

"Do you?" Her slender throat worked as she swallowed. Damn, but she looked vulnerable, gazing up at him. So vulnerable he wanted to pull her onto his lap and cuddle her, comfort her.

For starters.

"Have you ever taught anyone else to drive?"

"No, but I know I can do it. I am a very patient man, and never panic in emergencies, so there's no need for you to look so apprehensive." Was it apprehension causing her breasts to rise and fall so rapidly? Was fear responsible for that fluttery pulse in her throat? Or something else? Again, he had the uncanny sensation

that he should lift her into his arms, hold her close, reassure her. It was as if she were somehow begging him
to do it, though she'd looked down now and he couldn't
begin to guess at her emotions.

He shot to his feet and paced across the room. With
the safe distance of fifteen feet separating him from her
allure, he swept the drapes shut to close out the night.

"What worries you most about driving?"

She rose and began setting their cups onto the tray.

"I don't like cars."

"How can anyone not 'like' cars? What's the alternative?"

"Flying," she said so promptly and so positively he
had to chuckle.

"Well, it's one alternative, but only for long dis-
tances. It's not considered the best way to get to the
grocery store, unless your favorite supermarket is in
Memphis, Tennessee, and comes equipped with a run-
way."

Misty smiled, knowing he meant it as a joke. Was it
that he *wouldn't* believe, or couldn't? And why was it
so important to her that he overcame his resistance to
admitting what she really was? She'd dealt with other
mortals who refused to accept it. This time, though, it
troubled her more than it had ever before. She wanted
him to face the reality of her. Maybe then it would be
easier for her to accept what she now had to fight
against so hard she felt her energy levels depleting daily.

The cups on the tray rattled. "All right, fine," she
said, lifting her chin. "Let me fly, and I'll find a store
in Memphis, Tennessee, or maybe I'll shop in the agora
in Athens, or—"

His laugh interrupted her. "Misty, get serious. Nothing you say will change my mind. You'll like driving once you're used to it."

He exuded such confidence and certainty she felt almost convinced. Maybe she would like it, once she tried it. She loved driving carriages and created one for herself, with a pair of glossy black horses to pull it, whenever she visited an era when they were in use. But she could talk to a horse. How could she talk to an internal combustion engine?

The biggest obstacle to overcome would be proximity to him. Even here, in this big room, if he hadn't moved away when he went to close the drapes, she'd have ended up draping herself over him. She'd had an intense vision of herself curled on his lap, his arms around her, hers around him, their mouths locked together in a passionate kiss.

She noticed suddenly he was moving back toward her, though his feet had taken no steps. She forced herself to stop thinking of what it might be like to kiss him.

"What if I don't like driving?"

"All right, if you don't, then you can quit and I won't bring up the subject again. Fair enough? Listen," he said, lifting a strand of hair off her cheek and tucking it behind her ear, making her jump. If she didn't know better, she'd suspect him of magic. She hadn't even seen him coming and she knew perfectly well *she* hadn't brought him that close. Had she?

"If you're a nervous passenger, the best cure is learning to drive yourself. Then you can be in control," he said.

"I'm not nervous, and I'm always in control."

Are you, Misty? She stared blankly for a moment. Who had said that? *Are you in control now?*

"Yes!" she said aloud, and with emphasis.

He cocked an eyebrow. "So? What's the problem, then? Exactly what are you afraid of?"

"Cars are too small." The truth popped out because she had no option but to reply honestly.

"Small?" he echoed.

"Yes." The cups and saucers rattled again.

Alan took the tray from her. Most women, in his experience, preferred smaller vehicles. "The station wagon's not exactly a sports car, but if you'd rather take your lessons in a truck, I could—"

"A truck? Oh, no!" she yelped, and rushed away.

He followed her into the kitchen, watching the way her shimmery gown clung to her shape, revealing and concealing at the same time. He remembered the scent of her, and stepped closer to breathe it in again, reaching around her to set the tray down. She glanced at him over her shoulder, her mouth almost close enough to kiss. As he obeyed the impulse to do just that, she suddenly . . . wasn't there.

The back door swung slowly toward Alan and came to a rest, ajar. It must have created a faint breeze in moving, because suddenly a cold wash of goose bumps spread over his arms.

He switched on the outdoor lights and stepped outside.

Misty sat on Deanna's swing, her fingers clenched tightly around the plastic-coated chains. She'd squinched her eyes shut, compressed her lips and hunched her shoulders as if she were suffering intense pain.

"Misty, Misty, what's wrong?"

Clearly startled by the sound of his voice, she flung her head up, gaze flying to his face. "I'm still here?" It was close to a wail.

"Of course you're still here. Where did you expect to be?"

"Home. I just want to go...home."

"Home? What for?" And how in hell did she think she could do that sitting glued to a swing with her fists gripping the chains so tightly her knuckles were white?

"For... for a little while. To talk to the Mother. But the way is blocked. It's as if she's closed the door on me." She raised tragic eyes toward his face. "Oh, Alan, what if I can *never* go back?"

Disappointment slammed into him. She wanted to quit? Go back where she'd come from? Leave him? "Misty! Aren't you happy here?"

She dropped her chin toward her chest and shook her head, the back of her hair parting and draping forward around her neck. He looked down at her tender nape and couldn't help himself. He touched the softness of her skin, stroked his fingers over the little lumps of her vertebrae, then ceded to temptation and splayed his hand wide. He glided a stroking caress across her shoulder and past the short sleeve of her dress, to the satin texture of her arm, fingertips trailing all the way down to her wrist.

Crouching before her, he tilted her chin up and looked into her face. "Why Misty? What's making you unhappy?"

Her pointed chin trembled as she met his gaze. "You are."

Alan snatched his hand back. "I am? Why? How? Dammit, are you afraid of me?" He couldn't believe it.

"Me, the 'nice, harmless man who'd never do anything untoward?'"

"No, of course I'm not afraid of your harming me, not on purpose, but..." She blew upward, puffing her ragged bangs off her forehead. They fell back down in greater disarray. He itched to brush them straight, keeping his hands to himself with the utmost difficulty. "But a car is such a small place for me to be alone with you. I'll be able to smell you too much."

"Smell me?" Alan nearly fell over backward, but managed to catch onto the chains of the swing. It lurched, drawing her toward him, creating a dangerous situation. He shot to his feet and let her swing away.

"Good God! Do I stink?" He realized he was all but bellowing. Moderating his tone, if not his emotions, he said, "Have I got BO? Halitosis?" Jeez! He showered daily, brushed and flossed and visited his dentist regularly and—

"You smell good," she said in a small voice, cutting off his mental agonizing.

"I do?" He caught the chains again, holding her still. She nodded earnestly, looking up at him, forcing him to ask, "You don't like men who smell good?"

Her head bobbed again. "I like anything that smells good. Gingerbread. The ocean. Babies. Wild roses." She drew in a long breath and let it out slowly. "And you. Mostly you."

His breath escaped him in a rush. "What do I smell like?" He felt like a fool, asking, but there was nothing in the world that could have prevented the question, prevented the rapt way he leaned down to hear her whispered reply.

"Oh..." She paused, eyes half-closed, face dreamy, clearly considering it, and drew in a long breath, lifting her face toward him as if to savor his scent. His pulse went into overdrive. "You smell like a salty ocean breeze," she said, her voice little more than a thread of sound. "Like thick moss in the deepest forest. Like a herb garden. Like leather and—" She opened her eyes wide and gazed at him, took another deep breath. "There's more, but I can't decide what. It changes from moment to moment, and just being near you makes me need to breathe deeper and deeper to try to take it all in. I breathe so deeply I get dizzy, and when I get dizzy I can't think, and—" She broke off.

He tried to speak, made a weird croaking noise, cleared his throat and tried again. "And what?

"And it bothers me."

He let go, crouched again, grasping the seat of the swing, bent his head closer, drawing in her scent, wishing he could begin to identify some of its nuances. "Why, Misty? Why does it bother you?"

She dug one foot into the ground and pushed the swing away. "Because when I'm close to you I lose something. I like to be in charge of my faculties. All of them."

He caught the chains as she came back, holding her in place. He had to touch her. Cupping her cheek with one hand, he said, "Lose what?"

She closed her eyes. "My—" she swallowed visibly "—my abilities."

Her eyes fluttered open and her gaze met his. "When you touch me, I feel weak, Alan."

"Oh, Lord!" he breathed. "When I touch you I feel weak, too."

She nodded. "It's frightening. That's why I wanted to go home—to talk to the Mother, get some answers. I've never felt like this before."

"I don't think I have, either." He grasped her wrists and drew her hands from the swing chains, then tugged her till she stood before him. He brushed his thumb over her lower lip, feeling it tremble. "And the only answers we're going to find are within ourselves. The two of us. I want to kiss you, Misty."

A soft breeze lifted the pointed wisps of her bangs. Her eyes grew dark, almost black. "I'm afraid of what will happen if you do."

"So am I." He swallowed. "But are we going to let that stop us?"

Under his caressing thumb, her lips parted in a tremulous smile. "Elves are brave," she said. "We have to be. We get into lots of dangerous situations."

He smiled. He had to. She didn't look like a brave elf. She looked like a scared, virginal nanny in her brown dress and her wide-eyed uneasiness. *Brown dress?* Hadn't she been wearing— No. Imagination again. She also looked so very, very kissable he knew he could wait no longer. He bent and took her lips gently, carefully, as unthreateningly as he could manage . . . and the roof blew off the world.

She didn't kiss like a timid virgin. As she flowed against him, she didn't feel like she was afraid of anything, not the heat surging through them both like a live electric current, not the trembling in her limbs.

He groaned at the softness of her, at the firm resilience of muscle under satin skin. Unless his senses had completely deserted him, which was a possibility, Misty was definitely barefoot. The arch of her foot slowly slid the cuff of his trousers up the back of his leg. Her lips parted for him at his first hint he wanted them that way. She accepted the depth of his kiss, his exploring tongue, kissed him back in a way that told him she was no stranger to this kind of caress. Her breasts flattened against his chest, cushioning him as he pulled her ever closer. He ran one hand into her hair, fingers curving around the shape of her head. He thought he might die right there, holding her, kissing her, breathing in her sweetness, feeling her welcoming response.

Something uncontrollable grew and swelled in his chest, threatening to burst free. His knees trembled, his head spun and his eyes burned with a heat he could scarcely contain. Never in his life had he reacted to a kiss like this. It was holy, somehow, spiritual, and at the same time deeply sexy, totally arousing, and it filled him with a need he thought could never be met.

About to go under for the third time, he managed to gain a semblance of control. He tore his mouth free, threw back his head to gasp for breath, but couldn't release Misty completely. He needed to hold her close while he tried to calm down, gasping and puffing and blowing like a winded whale. "Misty," he sighed, moments later. "Oh, Lord, Misty."

She buried her face against his chest, breathing as raggedly as he did. Her fingers flexed rhythmically against the muscles of his back. Presently, she shivered, nestled closer.

He tried to wrap her entirely with his body. "Are you cold?"

"No." He just caught the faint whisper of sound. He lifted her chin and gazed into her face. Her lashes lay in dark arcs on her cheeks and, as he watched, they fluttered slowly open. They were real. He could see that now. Long, silky, curly...and all hers. She gazed at him for a moment through them, then lowered them again as a faint flush rose up over her cheeks. "I feel...strange. Warm. And...oh, I can't describe it.

Maybe if you kiss me again, I could think of the words to tell you what it makes me feel.''

He dropped his head. ''Misty,'' he whispered against her mouth. Her arms slid around his neck. Her lips trembled apart, and he swept the moist seam between them with the tip of his tongue. She welcomed him as she had before, returned what he gave, sought more, and he responded. In his arms, her body grew warmer, more pliant. Her breasts, taut, with pebbled nipples, pressed against his chest and that foot, seductive, soft soled, tantalizing, stroked his ankle, his calf. Never had anything felt more erotic.

He slid his hand down her back, over the swell of her hip and cupped her bottom, dragging her up onto her tiptoes, tight against his hardness. A ragged sigh rippled through her, and a deep shudder of pleasure, before she slid her arms from around his neck and settled back onto the soles of her feet.

He pulled back a few, very few, inches to look down at her.

''Oh, my,'' she said weakly, those incredible lashes fluttering open to reveal eyes shining with a dark, aroused glow. ''Oh, my goodness!'' She stepped back, let her hands trail slowly down his arms until she no longer touched him, and plopped down onto the seat of the swing again. She didn't struggle to describe anything this time, merely said, ''This should not be happening.''

''Maybe not, but it is.'' Crouching before her, he slipped his hand around the nape of her neck, under her hair, needing contact with her warmth again, to breathe in the sweet scent arising from her skin. He knew with certainty it was her scent this time; the phlox by the gate had finished blooming. It was her scent drifting around him that was addling his brain since the day she arrived.

Monday, Tuesday, Wednesday, Thursday. How his life had changed in less than a week!

He bent and dropped a quick kiss against the side of her neck. Lord! When he smelled her, he lost some of his abilities, too—the ability to breathe properly, the ability to think, the ability to reason. But not the ability to want her.

As he sucked in a harsh breath, she glanced up quickly, her lips parted in the beginnings of a question, or maybe a plea, or maybe no sound at all but another sigh. Alan knew he had to step away from her, step away now, before he completely lost it. He drew his hand back, stood shakily and staggered away to lean against the trunk of the apple tree. He had to stop rushing things like this.

"Now you see," she said, her voice startling him, forcing him to meet her gaze. "Now you see why I don't want to be alone with you in a car?"

He slowly lifted his head from where he'd rested it against the rough bark. "Misty—" He had to clear his throat. "Misty, do you think I'd take you out on some back road and molest you?"

She stared at him for a moment longer, then shook her head and rose her feet, a lustrous swirl of silk in many shades of purple swirling around her legs. The gown? Then where was the brown dress? Was he losing it entirely here?

"No," she whispered. "I think *I* might take you out on some back road and molest *you*."

6

"*YOU? MOLEST ME?*" Alan flung back his head and roared with laughter. It felt good, a release of some of his tension, and he let it go on long past the time when he should have stopped it, considering the furious glare she pinned him with, the threatening way she stepped toward him.

The mere thought of Misty "molesting" him made him forget not only why he should avoid close contact with her, but even that he'd ever thought there was a reason. He found himself within touching distance again, and naturally he touched her, just a gentle brush of a finger against her cheek, but it was enough to set him fully afire again.

"I figure I can look after myself," he lied. "If I didn't want to be molested, I wouldn't be."

"Yes," she said with a gravity that sent a sudden, cold shiver down his spine as he realized how serious she was. She backed away from him. "Yes, you would, if the Mother of All decreed it. She can't force *me*, but you don't have the same protection and your wanting me makes me . . . reckless. That's one place where fairies have it over us. They're so much more stable. Prissy, I've always called it, inhibited, but at least they know how to say no when they really believe they should.

"Which is most of the time," she added, not without a hint of disdain. "We elves are . . . different."

He almost said, *I'll say!* but bit his tongue. He didn't want to encourage her wonky beliefs. Exasperation both with her and himself stiffened his spine. "Misty, in the first place, I don't believe in your Mother of All. In the second place, even if I did, I wouldn't let some magical entity dictate to me."

"Oh, Alan . . ." She sadly shook her head. He hated the sorrow he saw in her eyes, wanted to eradicate it, wanted to kiss her again and again until not a shadow if it remained, nor a shadow of doubt in her mind, nor a hint of worry in her heart.

"You wouldn't be able to help it," she explained. "Or stop it, if that's what she wants. What if what you're feeling isn't real, but something she's induced?"

He thought she looked faintly pitying.

"It would be wrong of me to take advantage of you under those circumstances."

"Sweetheart . . ." He had to struggle not to laugh again at her earnest face, not to try to argue her out of her weird beliefs. What the hell was he doing, falling head over heels for a woman of unsound mind? Weren't there rules against it? Nevertheless, he felt as if it was his turn to take the next bungee jump and his feet were all tied up in elastic cords, holding him immobile. And if they hadn't been? Would he be running? Would he be taking so much as a single hop that might save him?

Nope!

This—whatever *this* was—felt a lot more compelling than any kind of common sense he might try to talk into himself.

He cradled her face in his hands, smoothing his thumbs over the planes and angles and curves of her features. Her cheeks were cool now, like porcelain, and her breath fluttered in and out raggedly. Dammit, why did she have to be such a total nut case? And why didn't it matter more to him that she was?

But really, was her belief that she was an elf created by the Mother of All any more irrational than a lot of religious tenets he'd run into? Such as, for instance, one that forbade children to laugh, to have toys or to make friends?

He didn't know the answer to those questions, but there was one whose answer he had no trouble discerning. "Sweetheart," he said again, "whoever, or whatever, is responsible for what kissing you makes me feel, I don't care. I like it. I want it, and I'm going to want a lot more of it. But if you need some time to get used to the idea, you've got it."

Her breath shuddered out again as she shook her head, dislodging his hands. She moved, glided— floated?—away from him until a good ten feet separated them. "I don't need time to get used to any idea," she said. "What you need is someone to steer you in the right direction. That's why I was sent. To find a woman to be Deanna's mother. Since you're her father, that woman must also be compatible with you—after all, she'll be your life companion. But that person is not me. Because I'm not really a person. I'm an elf."

She looked stern as she added, "With no aspirations toward permanent human form or life. We must both remember that."

"Wait a minute! Are you saying you think your task, the reason you were 'sent,' is to find me a wife?"

"Of course."

"Dammit, I don't want a wife! All I want is a nanny for my daughter. And, in you, that's what I have. I'm happy that way. I'm . . ." He let it trail off. To continue would be to continue a lie. It wasn't all he wanted. He wouldn't be happy with the status quo. Sure, he had a nanny for Dee, but he did want more. He wanted more of that nanny for himself.

She gazed at him. "You were saying?" Her tone indicated she knew the direction of his thoughts.

"Yeah. All right, so a nanny's not all I want. I want you. And unless I've forgotten how to read a woman's responses, you feel much the same way about me."

"But I'm not what you need, Alan. An . . . an association with me would not be good for you. That's what I'm trying to make you see. The Mother has interfered with this mission from the very first moment, and I do not understand why. I suppose she feels she can't trust me to handle it on my own, after the disastrous way I failed last time."

"Failed?"

"I was supposed to bring two people together."

"Were you an elf that time, too?"

Her quick indignation touched him oddly. "I'm always an elf," she said. "But that time, I took on the form of an Afghan hound."

Alan couldn't hold back a snort of laughter. It earned him a haughty glare. "Well, honey," he chortled, refusing to be intimidated by a woman who didn't quite come up to his chin, "no wonder you screwed up! I read a while back that Afghan hounds are the stupidest breed alive. They can't be taught even the simplest tricks."

She bristled, her chin rising, her lips firming, and took one step toward him. To his intense surprise, he backed up.

"They are not stupid!" she declared. "Of course they refuse to sit up, or to roll over and play dead. They're monarchs, Alan, so far above all that they can't be bothered. Why, I felt so regal and elegant when I took that form, I hated to change back. And the princess I lived with brushed me daily, sometimes three or four times a day, until my coat literally shone with good health. When we went walking, people stopped and stared, and watched me admiringly as I pranced beside my princess."

"No kidding." He propped his chin on his fist and crossed his ankles as he leaned his shoulder against the fence. He should encourage her to write some of these fantasies down. Cleaned up a little, made a tad more plausible, she might even make some money out of it. "Which princess was this?"

"Princess Aliea of Mandor. She saw Prince Hammigan's forty Afghans when she and her father visited him and his family in the kingdom of Larmel. She was captivated by the hounds and begged for one. The prince refused her request and she and her father left."

She frowned. "It was my task to bring the two young people together in order to unite the kingdoms, the better to withstand the Mongol hordes."

"Oh, I see. Mongol hordes. Buttercup, if you're going to continue in this storytelling hobby, take it from an expert who earns a living at the game. You need to read several books on how *not* to create trite situations and use cliché phrases. My editor would shoot me in the back of the head if I ever used a term such as 'Mongol hordes.'"

She ignored him, but her faint sniff told him she'd heard every word.

"I became an Afghan hound so the prince would have an extra animal and perhaps be more willing to share. I was quite certain he'd make her a gift of me, but instead, he was going to have me put to death because he wasn't certain of my lineage.

"Naturally, I ran away."

"Naturally." His tone was dry. "And ran right to the princess."

She smiled at him in that irritating way she had that made him feel like a first-grader who had just learned to sound out C-A-T. "Why, yes! I expected her to do the honorable thing and take me back to him. I believed that if only they saw a little more of each other, they'd do as their families hoped and fall in love. She did not send me back."

"I don't blame her. He was clearly a jerk. I mean, if I had forty dogs and a pretty girl wanted one, I think I'd share."

"Well, to be fair, it wasn't so much a case of his not wanting to share, but that they were breeding pairs and he needed to maintain the blood lines in a finely designed pattern to enhance the better traits and decrease the worst ones."

"Too bad it didn't work."

"What do you mean?"

"As I said before, Afghan hounds are too stupid to test."

"You know nothing about it! You've never been an Afghan hound, and I have."

Alan shut up. There was simply no way to argue with that. For sure, he had never been an Afghan hound.

"Why should any creature, but especially one who is royalty in her own right, dance to the tune of a mere human?" Misty continued scathingly. *"Pah!"*

" 'Pah?' Do people really say that?"

She poked her nose into the air. "I," she said, "am an elf."

"When you're not being a regal, elegant Afghan hound." Which she uncannily resembled in that moment.

She sniffed again. "That is all beside the point. The point is, I failed in my task that time, and because of that, the two kingdoms did not unite, but became bitter enemies, and a war broke out that went on for two generations until the Mongols came in and mopped up, wiping out what could have become a very powerful dynasty that would have contributed greatly to the culture of the day. And the future.

"The Mother was not pleased with me. She sent me back to school. When I finished my upgrading, she decided I was ready to try again."

Misty paced across the yard, past the sandbox and climbed the ladder of the slide. Sitting on top, she said, "This time, the Mother gave me what she said would be an easy assignment, but you're not making it so. Alan, truly, you must cooperate with me. We have to show the Mother that I am capable of managing your affairs without her intervention, or she'll never stop toying with us. She has me so discombobulated I don't suppose I could make any philters even if I had someone to make one for."

Alan followed her and stood at the base of the slide, looking up at her. She sat with her arms wrapped around her knees, her bare feet on the metal surface. He reached up and wrapped his hands around them, drawing her down toward him. "Philters?" He knelt on the bottom of the slide, placing her feet against his thighs. He felt their cold through the fabric of his jeans and covered them with his hands, rubbing gently, trying to warm them. "You make philters?"

"Of course." Her voice shook faintly. "I've been making philters for a very long time. Sometimes I even make an especially good one."

Oh, God! She kneaded with her toes in the same rhythmic, unconscious manner a cat kneaded with its paws, and it was about to drive him into a state of mania. Was he about to tell her to stop? Hah! He tried to keep his voice steady. "Is that a fact. And what constitutes a 'good' philter?"

"Naturally it's a fact. I told you, I never make false statements. A good one is one that works. One that gets the job done."

As he knelt there rubbing her feet, she went on to offer him a strange litany of other "facts" all having to do with her various accomplishments during previous stints spent on Earth, in earlier times when love potions were in common use. "Things are generally much, much easier in earlier periods of human history," she said. He thought he must be losing even more of his common sense, because her using the present tense for what was most assuredly the past, failed to bother him as much as he thought it should.

After all, this was Misty speaking. Whatever she said was bound to be weird. Entertaining, maybe, but definitely off the wall. Did he want her to stop talking? Never!

"The biggest problem with you is you have no one in your life," she went on in the manner of a kindly teacher explaining something to a not-too-bright student. "I simply don't know what to do, because, quite frankly, you have to begin dating women so I'll have some raw material to work with. There's no point in my mixing you a potion, or casting any spells, if there's no one in your life for me to cast them over, now is there?"

He laughed as he let her feet go and stood erect. She scooted to the bottom of the slide. Still chuckling, he sat on the swing. When she marched over to him ordering him to stop making light of a very serious situation, he reached out and snaked an arm around her waist, dragging her down onto his lap, where he held her while he continued to laugh.

"I think you've cast a spell over me, all right," he said against her hair when he finally sobered. "And in one of those delicious meals you've conjured up, you must have put in some kind of special potion, because you have me completely enchanted, Elf of the Morning Mist."

"But that's not my doing!" Misty wriggled in an attempt to free herself of his hold, but he held her captive and she found herself relaxing against him, breathing in the heady scent of his skin. She remembered vividly that there was a spot just under his ear where his flavor had been most intense. She ached to sample it again, and restrained herself with difficulty.

"That's what I'm trying to explain. It's not *my* spell you're reacting to, but the Mother's. And she's only doing it to jolt me into trying harder. I think I have it all figured out now. I see what she's up to. If I want you to forget about me, I'll have to ensure that you begin to think of someone else."

Alan grinned and ran his fingers into her hair, cupping her head in his hands. Part of her, a large part of her, liked it when he smiled at her in that intimate, half-sleepy way. Another part of her wanted badly not to like it. The mingling of feelings confused her, disconcerted her. All she could think to do was close her eyes.

That was a big mistake. She didn't even see him coming, so had no defenses up when he kissed her again.

"How could I possibly think of someone else *that* way?" he asked several moments later. Her head whirled and her ears roared so loudly she could just barely hear him. "When you're around, all I can think of is you, *that* way."

She managed to part her mouth from that tasty spot under his ear. After further exertion of will, she extricated herself from him completely. Taking one of the chairs at the patio table, she folded her arms across her chest and faced him. "Exactly!"

He rose from the swing and stepped toward her. "Exactly...what?"

"Stay there," she said, holding up a hand to ward him off. Whether her magic worked, or whether he chose to stay where he was, she didn't know. But at least he wasn't able to touch her from where he stood, nor was his scent able to agitate her to the point of insensibility, his taste about to elicit cravings she couldn't control.

"If you had other women around, you could begin to think of them in that way."

"Them?" he said. "Plural? Hey, now, I thought the object of this exercise was to find a mother for Deanna, not to procure a steady supply of popsies for me."

"It is. I mean, you'll probably need to date several, um, 'popsies' before you...choose."

"Hmm, I suppose you could be right. But there's a problem, Misty. I don't know any women I want to date. I'm not even sure I remember how to treat a woman on a date."

"Of course you do. Men don't forget things like that." She bit her lip. "Do they?"

He shrugged. "I seem to have." He looked at her slyly. "Maybe I should practice, say on you, before I try it with a real date."

"Whoa! I may be having a few problems with my abilities, but I'm not stupid. You just want to get me alone in your car where I can smell you."

He ran a hand through his hair, that grin of his tickling something deep inside her again. "I might think of a few other things you could do to me if we were alone in a car—or anywhere else—but that's certainly a novel idea. I'm serious about this, Misty. If you want me to start dating other women, then I need a few rehearsals. What about dinner together tomorrow night?"

"We have dinner together every night."

"This will be different. Just you and me. In a restaurant. Maybe some dancing afterward."

Dancing? Alan holding her in his arms? Their bodies moving together in time to slow, seductive music? Candlelight? Wine? "Maybe something chocolate for dessert?"

He grinned. "Sure. Whatever, uh, turns you on."

Misty realized she'd spoken that last sentence aloud, when she'd had every intention of internalizing it. "No!" she shouted, then gathered her scattered forces, concentrated hard, centered herself...and popped out.

7

MISTY SENSED Alan's consternation at her abrupt departure but it was nothing compared to her own. She'd badly miscalculated, and was now perched astride the roof of a neighbor's house. She must have made a noise upon landing because an elderly man rushed out into the yard, nightshirt flapping. He peered up at her. "What are you doing up there? I'm calling the police."

He disappeared back inside his house and Misty drew several long, deep breaths before she removed herself to a less exposed location.

Curled in the center of her bed, she considered conjuring up a soothing tune and a perfumed bower for herself. She knew, though, that nothing she could create in her present weakened state could compare to the memory of Alan's kisses, the taste of his mouth, the feel of his hard body, the sound of his rasping, laboring breath.

Or to the scent of his skin.

She didn't want to think of those things. She didn't want to remember the emotions he had evoked—intense, different from any she had ever experienced, awakening hungers in her she'd never fully understood. It wasn't fair.

She needed time to regroup, time to reassess. *She needed to go home.*

Right. She could do it. This minute. Only in the Upper World might she find an answer to her problems.

Problems. She'd never had problems like these, in all her six hundred plus years of experience. She'd had good assignments. She'd had better assignments, and she'd had that last, admittedly disastrous one. But never one like this. Never one where her powers were threatened.

Mother, I won't let you do this to me!

She huddled in the center of her bed, her throat tight with what she believed was rage until a sob broke through it and tears rained down her face. She crawled under the covers and cried till she'd washed away all the bad, frightened, confused feelings.

Then she lay on her back and smiled.

Dinner. Dancing. Candlelight. Wine. And something chocolate for dessert. None of those were reasons for tears. Or for fears. She was an elf, and elves could look after themselves.

"Bring on your dinner, Alan Magnus," she whispered. "Bring on your candlelight and wine. We'll see who wins at this little game you're playing, and I guarantee it won't be you."

For just a second, she allowed herself to think of how it would be if he did win, but quelled the thought almost as it was born. She gave her attention instead to considering the upcoming driving lessons, and fear pricked her again. She fought it down with soothing thoughts of chocolate mousse, a much safer outlet for her passions than Alan's kisses.

Right. He could even bring on his stupid automobiles, and she'd beat him at that game, too.

BY THE TIME Alan crossed the kitchen and entered the hallway, Misty had disappeared upstairs. He sighed. Up the stairs or...somewhere. Then he laughed at himself. He was not about to subscribe to her outrageous claims or let infatuation sway him from what he knew could be true, and what could not. For one thing, he knew she'd been in this very spot only moments before. A faint whiff of phlox-scented perfume hung in the air, but even as he recognized it, it faded into the night.

And for another thing, he told himself as he marched up the stairs to go to bed, she'd never been an Afghan hound, had never been an elf and she had not, absolutely had *not,* disappeared from the backyard, leaving him staring at a tiny wisp of mist. He was tired, and it was way past his bedtime.

Nor was he infatuated. A better choice of word was "fascinated." But even life-threateningly dangerous things could fascinate. A man simply had to keep his desires in check along with his imagination.

Writers, he knew, were much too given to flights of fancy, especially when the current book was all but done and their minds began casting around desperately for the next idea to work up into a story. He was no more immune than the next guy.

He stripped and stepped into the shower, standing still as the hot spray pelted his skin. Was that what this was all about? Having switched from writing mysteries to thrillers, was he now being pushed in the direction of fantasy?

He hoped not. His agent had been upset enough by the one switch.

He'd just have to get a grip on himself and keep a firmer rein on his imagination. Except, dammit, he was a writer. Writers weren't supposed to curb their bent toward the fanciful.

Not even to stop themselves believing in disappearing nannies?

Right. There, he would draw the line. Nannies did not disappear. Elves did not become nannies, and no one became an Afghan hound! Ever.

And he'd do both himself and Misty a favor—he'd tell her first thing in the morning the dinner date was off. He'd stay away from her, never kiss her again, stop thinking of her as anything but a nanny and, yes, he'd start dating other women. Soon. Really, really soon. Maybe even tomorrow.

Mark had extras. He was always willing to share. Right. Tomorrow was Friday. What better night than Friday for a pub crawl with his best buddy and a couple of friendly women? Unless it was Saturday night. So why not do both?

FRIDAY EVENING, as he readied himself to go out, he remembered he hadn't yet discussed her time off with Misty. Well, never mind. He'd do that, too, but not until he'd had a couple of nights out himself. It was safer that way, safer not to be alone with her, safer not to so much as acknowledge her presence when Deanna was fast asleep.

As he left his room, he saw Misty's door was closed. He briefly considered telling her he was leaving, but he'd already mentioned at dinner that he'd be going out for the evening.

She'd merely shrugged, which told him she didn't care one way or another, and said, "Have a nice time, Alan. I won't wait up."

Hmmph! As if he'd asked her to.

She obviously hadn't taken very seriously his suggestion that the two of them have dinner out somewhere together so he could "practice" dating, because when he didn't mention it, neither did she. She also had dinner on the table at the usual hour as if she'd had no expectation of being taken out.

Also as usual, it beat anything he could have ordered for them in the finest restaurant in town. But there was nothing chocolate for dessert.

His evening out with Mark and two women was pleasant enough. To a point. They barhopped for a while, then went to Richards on Richards, where Mark was one of the lucky ones who never had to stand in line, and then went back to Mark's place. They sat in the hot tub on the deck, discussing topics of little interest to Alan, and he nearly fell asleep right there, until the woman who was supposed to be "his" ran her bare foot up the back of his leg.

He jerked away, sat up straight and announced he had to get home and could he offer the two ladies a ride. Both declined. They lived in Mark's apartment complex. The one with the foot suggested that if he was tired and needed a little "rest" before his long trip home, she had room for him.

He wasn't *that* tired.

As he drove across Lions Gate Bridge, looking out at the lights of the North Shore, he remembered how Misty's foot sliding up his calf had produced such a different effect from Linda's. He thought her name was Linda. Damn. Or was it Lois? He'd have to ask Mark, because the four of them were going to a beach party on Bowen Island the next day.

He hoped she'd keep her feet to herself, to say nothing of other portions of her anatomy. He wasn't a prude by any means, but dammit, he'd just met her that night. He didn't take liberties with women he didn't know, and figured they should do likewise.

But what about "liberties" with a woman he did know? The thought popped into his mind as he opened the front door and stepped through. Yes!

No! He corrected himself at once. He was glad to get home, that was all, and it had nothing to do with the unique scent he fancied had pervaded the house in the past few days. When he stood in the foyer, leaning on the door, breathing deeply, it was nothing more than the peace and serenity of his own home that welcomed him. He'd do well to remember it was only peaceful and serene because Misty was sound asleep. When she was not, even if they were in separate rooms, stirred up, seriously agitated or on edge more accurately described his state of mind. Which probably had a great deal to do with his adverse reaction to Linda's bare foot on his calf tonight.

Linda? Lisa? Lydia? He sighed and shrugged. It scarcely mattered, did it? Mark would remember the woman's name. Mark had a knack for that. The same as Misty had a knack for disturbing the hell out of him.

Quietly Alan ascended the stairs with Misty on the brain—memories of Misty's pansy eyes and her soft, solemn voice saying, *Elves don't need cars. We fly.*

He'd almost bought into that, the night he'd kissed her. He'd closed his eyes for what had felt like only a second, and when he'd opened them, she was gone, for all the world as if she really had flown away.

But dammit, he was not a fanciful man. Misty might have a capricious sense of humor and take some strange kind of pleasure in pretending she was an elf, but he, on the other hand, did not like to pretend things, especially not to himself. He took great care, despite his profession—maybe even because of his profession—to keep his everyday life firmly rooted in reality.

That had been the one thing he wished he'd been able to make his father see, he thought, pausing briefly outside Misty's door, drawing in another breath of her scent.

For a moment, he thought he heard faint strains of music—panpipes. He froze, remembering the house cleaner and her "little, naked man with horns and hooves," but when he stopped and listened harder, the sounds had disappeared. Just another manifestation of his overactive imagination. He could almost hear his father's dry, precise tones suggesting that he curb it.

Opening Deanna's door, he tiptoed to her bed and stood looking down at her sweet, sleeping face. He loved her more than he'd ever thought it possible for him to love anyone. He had such hopes for her.

Was this what his father had felt when he stood looking down at his sleeping children, assuming he ever had? No, let's get realistic, Alan demanded of himself. Had his father ever stood looking down at his sleeping *son,* filled with unarticulated hopes?

No, just with unfulfilled wishes. But at least Brigadier General Magnus hadn't been disappointed by his *daughter*—like he had been with Alan, and the realization still had the power to sting him.

"Put away the make-believe, and get on with a *man's* life," he'd urged. "You'll never support a wife and family by sitting indoors scribbling in a book. Imagination doesn't win the battles a man has to win to live successfully in this world. I didn't raise you to be a dilettante."

No. His father had raised him to be a soldier, expected him to be a soldier, prepared him for the military life. But all the military history drummed into his head, all those hours of drilling on sunbaked, snow-covered or rain-drenched parade squares, all the pomp and ceremony and uniforms and discipline of military academy, couldn't quell an imagination that simply refused to be quelled.

Instead, Alan quit the military, trading in the crisp uniform for sloppy sweats. He exchanged the "promising" military career for an uncertain future. Instead of a "decent" haircut, Alan went around shaggy half the time because he was too lost in his current book plot to remember there was another world out there. One in which his father lived; the only one in which his father could believe or trust.

Despite the success Alan had eventually enjoyed, despite his proving he could be as practical as he was imaginative, his father had never fully forgiven him.

His mother had revealed, though, after Dad's funeral, that he'd read every one of Alan's books, over and over.

Now, before letting himself silently out of his daughter's room, Alan renewed a vow he'd made shortly after he'd brought Deanna home—he would never fail to tell her he was proud of her. Not even when she disappointed him.

As he went to bed, he again thought he heard the reedy sound of panpipes. Quickly, he pulled a pillow over his head and renewed an even earlier promise to himself—no one would ever be able to accuse him of allowing fiction to overshadow reality.

Misty was not an elf, and she did not have some little Grecian god in her room playing her a lullaby.

WEDNESDAY EVENING, Misty had just gotten comfortable when Alan knocked lightly on her door. Without even having to exercise her increasingly unreliable powers, she knew who it was. For one thing, Deanna was in bed. For another...she just knew. She stood from the mossy couch she'd created in one corner of her sitting room and smoothed down her gown.

Quickly, she sent the couch, the waterfall and the goldfish pond back to the Upper World, and deflected the warm sun she'd had shining on the trees for the benefit of the baby birds in their nests. Then, lest they start peeping, she sent them home, too, along with their sunbeam.

It was a good thing she'd done all her clearing up before opening the door, because as she did, her knees went weak and her head whirled. Magic, other than the magic of Alan's presence, would have been impossible. Something inside her turned over; her eyelids grew heavy and her heart pounded with painful slowness.

She tried to speak but couldn't form a single word. She could only look into Alan's eyes, seeing desire and confusion there.

"Hi," he said, his voice sounding rusty, as if he hadn't used it for weeks.

She swallowed before she could reply. "Hi."

"Uh, I hope I'm not disturbing you."

Disturbing her? Oh, if only he knew! Misty tried not to breathe too deeply as Alan's scent swirled around her, threatening to jumble her brain permanently instead of just sending her flopping across someone's roof.

"Do you play chess?"

"Chess?" She had been too busy trying to hold herself together to sense that one coming.

"Yes, chess. You know, with kings, queens, pawns, all that?"

"I know what chess is. Yes. I play."

"Good. If you're not too tired, we could..." He shrugged. "If you like, we could have a game. Or two."

"Oh!" She'd half expected him to announce that during the weekend he had found a woman and wanted Misty to cast a spell or brew a special potion. She'd already decided that when he did, she'd check out the woman herself. Just to make sure he'd found a good mother for Deanna.

"No kissing?"

His eyes widened for a second. "Um..."

"I can't let you kiss me again, Alan. It's not good for me."

"I don't think it's particularly good for me, either, at least not just leaving it at a kiss or two. But if that's what you want, you've got it. No kissing, just chess."

"Okay," she replied, then bit her lip. *No* was the answer she should have given. *No* was the answer she would have given, if only she were able to lie.

As she pulled the door shut behind her and drank in the sight of his smile, she blurted out, "I think it's only fair to warn you, though—Attila taught me to play."

He tilted his head as he looked down at her and draped his arm over her shoulders, steering her toward the stairs. "Attila?

"The Hun."

He grinned, sighed and shook his head, then snatched his arm back. Her shoulders felt cold as she followed him down to the first floor.

"Would you like some coffee and cookies?" she asked.

"I'll get them," he said. "If you'll tell me where the cookies are. I went searching a while ago and couldn't find them."

Misty suppressed a smile. "If I told you where I keep the cookies, you wouldn't need me anymore."

His expression went sober. "Don't bet the farm on that one, Misty. You've made yourself pretty well indispensable."

"Everyone's dispensable," she said, but knew he could search the kitchen all night and never find so much as a cookie crumb. She'd have to take to leaving some in the canister at all times, considering how much he liked them.

If she could. She couldn't even begin to start making tonight's cookies until she was a good ten feet away from him with a door shut between them.

When she arrived in the living room he had the chessboard set up. He flipped a coin to see who went first, asking for her guess as the coin spun down. Misty cheated and peeked. She always preferred to play black.

An hour later, he wiped imaginary sweat from his brow and said, "I think I believe you!"

"About?"

"Learning chess from Attila the Hun. You're deadly. And," he added, narrowing his eyes, "I have a nasty hunch you let me win that last game."

Misty smiled. As long as it was only a hunch. "Do you ever play Go?"

He grinned. "*Do* I? Now, there, I warn you, I'm the deadly one. But let's save that for tomorrow. Want another game of chess?"

Before she could reply, the doorbell rang. She rose to her knees from where she'd been curled beside the coffee table, wondering if it was a nanny's place to go to the door.

"Huh? Who would that be?" Alan asked, glancing at his watch.

"It's your mother," she said, because he had asked.

"My—" He broke off, shook his head hard, giving her one of those half skeptical, half amused smiles of his, his mouth quirking up on one corner. "What makes you say that? She's not due back till next week."

She shrugged. "Nevertheless, it's her."

With an impatient sound, he strode out in response to another pealing of the bell. As she put the chess game away, knowing they wouldn't be playing again that evening, Misty heard his amazed, rather crude exclamation, followed by a feminine laugh that segued into a chiding tone. "Well, yes, you're a son, but certainly no son of mine could be described as a son of *that*."

Alan's mother then said something about them missing their own bed, and the door thudded shut. "After I tucked Christopher in, I felt restless, so here I am," she was saying as Alan returned, her arm through his.

It wasn't that her slender height, the silver swirls through her cap of short, dark curls or her bright blue, inquisitive eyes intimidated Misty. Little if anything did that. Nevertheless, she took a step back, struck by the power and confidence this woman emitted. In her navy pantsuit with a beautifully cut jacket over a bright red sweater, she looked as if she'd just stepped straight out of her dressing room rather than off a long, international flight.

Alan's face wore a partly chagrined, partly annoyed expression as he met Misty's gaze. "You were right," he said. "You must be psychic."

"I am."

He compressed his lips, but didn't argue.

"Mom, this is Misty Fawkes. Misty, my mother, Janet Rankin."

"Well, now!" Mrs. Rankin's candidly curious gaze swept over Misty again. "Where did *you* come from?"

Misty wished she hadn't asked, but since she had, there was no choice but to answer honestly. "From the Upper—" she began, but Alan swiftly interrupted.

"The upper, uh, upper Fraser Valley," he finished for her. "Agassiz, if I recall it right. A lovely place, Agassiz, isn't it, Mom?" He thrust the plate of cookies toward his mother. "Have one. Have two or three. Misty made them. She's an incredible cook. Keeps the kitchen filled with delicious aromas. Remember, we had lunch there once? Agassiz, I mean, not the kitchen." His laugh sounded lame, but he rushed right on. "Imagine! We might even have been in the same restaurant as Misty that day. Misty, did you ever have lunch in Gianni's Taverna in Agassiz?"

Misty stared at him. "No, Alan. I never did."

"Well, darn! Then I guess we couldn't have shared the place with you, after all. We'll all have to drive up there for lunch one day, right after I get my revisions completed. Do you like pizza, Misty? Mom and Chris, her husband, both do, and so do Deanna and I. Maybe you could fix pizza for us one night. Or, if you'd rather, we could order in. We—"

"Alan! For goodness' sake, what's the matter with you? You're babbling like a lunatic." His mother fixed him with an inquiring stare. "I haven't seen you this agitated since I caught you with your telescope on Kimberley Laketon's bedroom window."

He gaped at her. "You *caught* me? You *knew?* But I—I told you I was looking at the stars."

She laughed indulgently. "Really, Alan. It was a cloudy Christmas night and you were fourteen years old. You blushed and babbled in your anxiety to get your telescope covered up and out of my sight."

He covered his eyes with one hand, half laughing. "Oh, cripes!" Then, fixing his mother with a questioning stare, he asked, "Why the hell didn't you tell me you knew? I've spent years feeling guilty about that, you know."

"Guilty and embarrassed, I sincerely hope, as well as much chastened. However, just in case you weren't chastened enough, I suggested casually to Mrs. Lake-ton that she tell Kim to make sure her drapes were closed as long as you were home from school, so you weren't tempted again."

"You told Mrs. Laketon?" His voice rose. "She told *Kim?* I..." Alan clacked his mouth shut, shook his head and sank onto the love seat. "Did you tell Major Lake-ton, too?" He almost looked fourteen again.

Misty tried hard to contain her laughter, but failed. He glared at her. "Why don't you go get another cup, then we can all have coffee."

"Go and get it yourself," his mother ordered. "I want to get to know this girl. You've been blathering on so much she's hardly had a chance to say hello."

"*I've* been blathering on? What about—"

His mother ignored him as she held out her hand to Misty. With her eyes twinkling, she winked. "My, but you are a pretty little thing, aren't you?"

Misty glanced in a mirror over the mantel. "Why, yes, I am."

Mrs. Rankin chuckled, looking suddenly very much like her son. "And modest, too, I see."

"Modest? Oh, no."

Fairies might be self-effacing and diffident, but elves knew who they were, and what they were, and took pride in their accomplishments. She was pleased the persona she had created as Deanna's nanny appeared pretty to others. It was what she'd aimed at. Children responded much more positively to beauty than they did to its opposite.

"It's not my way to be modest."

The chuckle escalated into delighted laughter. "So I see. How—" Mrs. Rankin pursed her lips "—how interesting. I think I'm going to like you."

"Thank you. I know I'll like you. You resemble your son."

Mrs. Rankin shot Alan an amused glance. "Backward thinking, my dear," she said to Misty. "*He* resembles *me*."

"Of course."

"I'm so glad you found someone, son." Looking back at Misty, she added, "Welcome. I'm delighted to meet you."

"And I, you, Mrs. Rankin. I hope you had a good trip home."

"We did, thank you, but it's a long flight from New Zealand. We should have broken it in Hawaii." She smiled at Alan as she let Misty's hand go. "We would have, but we missed our princess too much. How is she?"

"Wonderful," Alan replied. "She missed you, too."

"I don't suppose you did, though. Or not much, anyway."

"Well, let's us sit down, too, since my rude son is already doing so." Mrs. Rankin spun around and lowered her long, lean shape onto an upholstered chair, then leaned toward Alan.

"I know it's late and I should have gone straight to bed after arriving home from the airport, but I slept well on the plane, and I saw your lights on. I have a million things to tell you, Alan." She cut her gaze sideways toward Misty, still standing, and added, "As it seems you two must have a few to tell me."

"Mom!" Alan's laughter had a hollow ring. "This isn't what you think it is, despite Misty's, er, despite the way she's dressed. She's Deanna's new nanny, not my, uh . . . She's the *nanny*. Nothing more. Tell her Misty!"

"I'm the nanny."

Mrs. Rankin blinked slowly, glancing between the two of them. "I see." Misty sensed her disappointment. "Well, this may be even more of an unexpected event, then. The last time I talked to you, Alan, you'd all but given up on finding anyone."

She smiled at Misty again, with no less interest. "Sit down, my dear, please. I want to know all about you. When did you come? How do you and my granddaughter get along?"

"I came a week ago Monday, Mrs. Rankin. Deanna and I get along very well."

"She is a darling, isn't she?"

"Yes, Mrs. Rankin."

"Sit down, sit down," Alan's mother urged again, but Alan's emotions, a swirling aura of perturbation, urged her the other direction.

"Thank you, but I'm sure you and your son have a lot to discuss. I'll leave you now, if you don't mind."

"I do mind." Mrs. Rankin was nothing if not direct. "Of course we have a lot to discuss, but you're part of it." She grinned. "Surely you don't want us doing it behind your back?"

"I..." Misty blinked, suddenly not certain how to respond to that. They could only discuss her behind her back with her compliance. If she were the topic of discussion, she had no compunctions about listening in; she had plenty of options. She could make herself invisible; she could become a tiny spider no one would see on the draperies; or she could even place herself inside the coffeepot and peek out the spout. They'd never notice her in the steam.

Alan laughed and stood. "Well! For once, I see you're speechless." To Misty's dismay, he wrapped his arm around her shoulders again and turned her toward the love seat. His reluctance to sharing his mother with her seemed to have evaporated in the past few seconds. His aura now glowed a healthy, positive blue as he asked, "Is there enough coffee in that pot for three?"

Misty nodded. In fact, there was enough coffee in the pot for ten, a hundred, more. It would stay full until she decreed otherwise. Unless Alan touched her too often, then it might go empty, the coffee might become lemonade, or the pot could turn into an elephant, for all the control she'd have over things.

"Mom," Alan said, "you're not permitted to tell Misty one more embarrassing secret out of my past. Understand?"

She laughed. He left, presumably to get another cup, but was back so fast Misty again almost suspected him of performing magic.

"I waited till you got back to continue with the embarrassing boyhood stories," his mother said. She winked at Misty. "Believe me, it's true when they say boys will be boys. He also had a massive crush on his fifth-grade teacher, and became quite inarticulate whenever anyone mentioned her name."

Misty laughed again. "Did he blush then, too?"

"Exactly the way he is now. He was so sweet, my dear. You'd have liked him as a boy. Everyone did. I knew from about his third birthday that he was destined to be a charmer and a heartbreaker. He's done more than his fair share of that. Oh, there are stories I could tell you that would—"

She broke off, shaking her head. "But never mind. You look like a girl who can hold her own, and as far as I'm concerned, it's high time my son had someone who—"

"Mother!" It was a bellow of outraged male dignity.

She looked startled, innocent. "What?"

"Would you quit talking about me as if I'm not here?"

He sat again, heavily, beside Misty, who glanced apprehensively at the coffeepot. Everything was in order. No elephants, at least. And the steam still smelled like coffee. She tightened her focus.

"And there's no need for my childhood history," Alan continued. "I told you, Misty is Dee's nanny. Nothing more."

"Oh, all right, if you insist." Her smile made it clear she remained unconvinced. "My mistake. I was fooled by that very lovely wisp of lingerie Misty's wearing." Her grin would have done the Mother proud. "It gives an obviously false impression of . . . intimacy."

Alan reared back. "It's not a wisp and it's not lingerie and there's no intimacies this evening. I promised Mist—" He choked the words off with a cough and cast a long look over Misty. "That, er, gown covers her from her collarbone to her toes. It's not the slightest bit revealing, unless a person has a vivid imagination and a dirty mind."

He closed his eyes and took a deep breath, which he held for an alarming length of time. Misty considered poking him in the side with an elbow to facilitate its release, but as the thought formed, the breath escaped him in a loud gust.

"Have some coffee," he said, and filled all three cups.

"Alan, I approve of her," his mother said reassuringly. "Please don't feel you need to explain or try to justify your actions. I'm truly delighted that Misty has come to live with you." She smiled at him and stirred cream into her coffee.

"She's not living with me! Not in that sense. She's—"

"Deanna's nanny. I know. You've told me several times. I must add, though, she's an unexpected treat.

"You may not know it," she went on, turning to Misty, "but my son appeared determined to hire an elderly or middle-aged nanny for Dee. I tried to tell him he was wrong, that both he and Deanna needed someone young and vital in their lives, but would he listen? Not on a bet."

"I think he understands that now, Mrs. Rankin."

"Good. And call me Jan. I think we're going to become friends."

Misty smiled. "I hope so, Jan. I enjoy having friends. So far, I have only Deanna and Alan, here on Earth. And now you."

The phone rang in Alan's study. He stiffened, but stayed put, eyes fixed on his mother's face. The phone rang again, shrill, urgent.

"Well? Aren't you going to answer that?" Jan asked. She glanced at her watch. "Must be important, this time of night."

He stood, still clearly unwilling to leave the two of them alone together. "I . . . It's probably a wrong number."

"Don't be silly. Go and answer it. We'll be fine here, the two of us. Go on, Alan." She dismissed him with a wave of her hand, saying, "Shoo!"

He made a frustrated growling sound, cast a last, desperate glance stabbing into Misty's eyes and lunged out of the room.

8

JAN SMILED at Misty and said, "So...you like my son, do you?"

"Oh, yes. I like your son very much."

Jan sipped, regarding Misty over the rim of her cup. "I'm glad you said that." She selected a cookie, took a bite, chewed and swallowed, then set the remainder of it on the edge of her saucer. "I wouldn't ordinarily mention a subject as delicate as this on so short an acquaintance, but you and I might not have many opportunities to speak alone. You may not have been here very long, but I sense there's already...something in the air. He likes you, too. I could tell at a glance."

Her intense blue gaze sharpened. "My son is very important to me."

Misty nodded.

"Alan needs a wife," Jan said. "Are you aware of that?"

"Yes, I am."

"Which is more than he is."

Once more, Misty nodded in agreement.

"I intend to see that he gets one," Jan continued. "With or without his cooperation."

"Good," Misty said, smiling. "Then we're on the same wavelength because that's my intention, too."

Jan leaned back in her chair, kicked off one shoe, hooked her heel on the edge of the cushion and folded her arms atop her bent knee. She gave Misty a long, speculative look. "May I speak frankly to you, Misty?"

"Of course." People always spoke frankly to her. It was part of her being an elf. They couldn't help themselves, and often astounded themselves with the secrets they revealed. Misty tried hard to keep people at their ease, to make them not mind the things they said to her, but it wasn't always possible.

"I've been trying to find someone for him for the past five years. Longer, actually. But to no avail." Jan smiled wryly. "Both my children appear to consider themselves more cut out for the single life. Until Deanna came on the scene, I'd all but given up on the idea of grandchildren. I wasn't even aware Alan had ever had a special relationship with a woman. I'm delighted to have a granddaughter, of course. It's just that I want...more for Alan."

She fell silent. Misty waited, knowing she had more to say.

Jan cleared her throat. "Since it's obvious to me that Alan is intrigued with you, I have to ask what your intentions are."

She blinked, then frowned. Misty sensed those weren't the words she'd expected to utter. "I mean—" She chopped off the sentence, as if she was suddenly unsure exactly what it was she did mean.

"I understand," Misty said. "My intentions are to find someone to fill the gap in Deanna and Alan's life."

"Someone such as yourself?" While Jan Rankin might be pleased to know Alan was "intrigued" by Misty, clearly she wasn't without reservations. "Don't you think you're too young for him?"

"No," Misty replied in complete honesty. "Nor do I see myself as the one for him."

"Really." Jan planted her foot back onto the carpet and sat forward, frowning. "Then who?"

"That remains uncertain. He doesn't seem to have any women friends for me to work on."

"Yes. I know just what you're saying. But I'd hate to see either Deanna or Alan grow attached to someone who didn't plan to be in their lives a long time."

"So would I. Deanna needs a mother as much as Alan needs a wife. It's my mission to find someone to fill both roles."

Jan's eyes widened. "Your *mission?*"

"Yes. I came because they need me. When they no longer have that need, I'll leave. But not before I leave them in good hands. In the meantime, I'll do everything in my power to make them happy and keep them healthy."

"That's good to hear. How much—"

"Well, now!" Alan came back into the room and plopped down beside Misty. "How are you two getting along?" he asked as he bent forward to grab a cookie off the plate on the coffee table.

"Very well," Jan said. "I was just going to ask Misty about some of her other experiences as a nanny."

"Experience? Oh, Misty's had lots of experience," he said expansively. "Something like fifteen years, I believe." He spoke so quickly Misty knew he was afraid she would say something to embarrass him. Didn't he understand, unless someone asked her directly, as he had done, she wasn't about to reveal herself?

Jan raised her brows. "Fifteen years? My goodness. You must be considerably older than you look."

"Yes," Misty agreed, straight-faced. Then genuine curiosity compelled her to ask, "How old do I look?"

"Around twenty."

Misty shrugged. "Close enough, I suppose. I was trying for thirty-five."

Jan looked mystified. "Trying for...?"

Alan began choking on a mouthful of cookie and grabbed for his coffee cup. His mother leapt up and began pounding him on the back.

"Twenty is hardly close to thirty-five in most women's books," Jan observed, resuming her line of questioning once Alan quieted down, "unless you're looking at it from the perspective of seventy or eighty years. Then, I'm told, anything under forty seems nubile."

"Oh." Misty frowned. Maybe the difference between twenty and thirty-five *was* vast here. She sighed. "I thought I looked thirty-five in my brown shoes and green dress."

"Oh, easily," Alan cut in quickly. "At least thirty-five. Maybe more. Very nannylike. In your green dress and brown shoes." His tone indicated his low opinion of that costume.

"You certainly can't say that about the sexy little number she has on now."

Alan's gaze swept over Misty, and lingered here and there before he said briskly, "It's not a sexy little num—"

"Of course it is," his mother interrupted. "And don't pretend you haven't noticed." She laughed, obviously enjoying teasing her son. "In it, Misty could be anywhere between eighteen and twenty-two, but not a day older."

"Looks," Alan said, his gaze fixed on Misty's face, "can be deceiving."

"That is truly a beautiful fabric." Jan touched Misty's gown, rubbing the cloth between thumb and forefinger. "Pure silk. I should have known. Nothing else can come close to it for quality. You must have searched hard to find shades that so exactly match your eyes. Mind my asking where you got it?"

"I made it."

Jan's eyes widened appreciatively. "I've never seen a pattern for such a unique design. Or did you design it yourself?"

"Yes."

"Well! You must have a good eye, as well as clever fingers."

"Misty's extremely clever," Alan cut in swiftly, plucking at a fold of her gown, rubbing it between his fingers much as his mother had done, then smoothing it back out on her leg. "She made a puppet out of Deanna's toy dog. The two of them play with it all the time. It looks and sounds so real it's hard to believe it isn't. And her cooking . . ."

His voice faded out behind the roaring in Misty's ears. She went totally still as his thumb stroked over the silk covering her thigh. Her skin burned. His thumb swirled one direction, his fingers the other, making tiny, sensuous circles as if he were completely unaware of what he did, unaware of what his touch did to her.

She concentrated, focused, willed his hand away, but nothing happened. The gentle touch persisted as he continued speaking. She knew he spoke, because his lips, firm, beautifully chiseled above his square chin, moved, but she heard nothing, watching in mesmerized fascination as he smiled at his mother, then turned and smiled at her.

With enormous strength of will bred in desperation, Misty gathered herself, centered herself and . . . left.

"AAAK!" JAN SHOT to her feet, staring frantically around. "Where the hell did she go?"

Alan nearly leapt out of his skin when his mother yelped and he became sickeningly aware of the warm, empty spot where Misty had sat only an eye blink before. With supreme effort, he pretended nothing was wrong. "Go? Who?"

Pretended? He wasn't pretending. Nothing was wrong. It couldn't be.

"Misty. Deanna's nanny." Jan rubbed her upper arms briskly as if to erase goose bumps and sat again. "If I hadn't seen it with my own eyes, I'd never have believed it. One minute she was sitting there and you were stroking her leg, and then the next minute she was . . . gone."

"Stroking her leg? I wasn't stroke—" Had he been? Oh, Lord...the sensation of silk, the feel of warm, firm flesh under it and— Help! Lord help him, he had been stroking her leg and she had simply...gone. How could she do that to him?

The fact was, she couldn't do any such thing. He and his mother were both overtired. Most likely hallucinating. Maybe he'd even hallucinated Misty from the very beginning, hallucinated his parents' return from their vacation, hallucinated the coffee, the cookies, Misty's warm thigh and—

No. That part, especially that part, of this whole bizarre sequence was real, if none of the rest was. And if Misty had been there, and then wasn't, it was because she had slipped away when neither he nor his mother had been paying attention.

Hah! He was a man. Misty had been in the room. Ergo, he had been paying attention to her. But...she did move quickly sometimes. And she did move quietly. That was all. There was nothing odd about her departure. There was no earthly reason for the chill that prickled his arms and the back of his neck.

No *earthly* reason . . .

In an effort to convince both himself and his mother that there was nothing odd going on, Alan refilled their cups, set the pot down, frowned, then lifted it again, experimentally. It was pretty heavy for a pot that had already dispensed five full cups. Setting it down, he checked inside. Almost full, and still emitting steam. He swirled it around to be sure, and then blinked as the swirling fluid subsided, leaving only an inch in the bottom.

Startled, he almost dropped it—the almost full pot had clearly been an optical illusion. He remembered the weight of it. And a tactile one? Was there such a thing as a tactile illusion?

Still reeling, he had to take another gulp of coffee before he could speak again. "Mom, I think you're more exhausted than you believe. Misty said good-night ten minutes ago."

His mother stared at him. She didn't believe a word he'd said. Hell, *he* didn't believe a word of it, but it could possibly be true, couldn't it? It was, surely, a better explanation than any other he could come up with. Warming to his subject, he expanded on it. "I was, um, telling you how, with Misty to take care of Dee, I finally got my revisions finished and sent them away yesterday, then all of a sudden you shouted and scared me half to death."

He managed a smile he hoped was convincing and rose to his feet, stepped around the coffee table and held out his hands to her. "Come on. You're tired and jet lagged and, as you said when you arrived, you need your own bed. Did you walk over, or drive?"

She stared for a long moment at the spot where Misty had been sitting, obviously not fully convinced she hadn't seen what they both knew they couldn't truly have seen. "All right," she said, letting him pull her up. "I guess I am more tired than I thought if I let myself become so distracted I didn't see Misty leave, or say good-night to her. Sorry about that."

She grimaced. "Things like this happen when you start to age."

He laughed. "You're not quite sixty, Mom. Hardly 'aged.' And I've never seen you looking better, despite all those hours in transit."

"Nevertheless . . ." She glanced again at the empty seat. "An intriguing girl, your new . . . nanny," she said. "Not at all what I thought you wanted."

He gnawed on his lower lip for a moment, then shrugged. "She's not what I thought we needed. But Dee fell for her in five seconds flat."

"Dee, huh?"

He glanced sharply at his mother's face. "What does that mean?"

"I think you can figure it out," his mother said dryly. "Dee's not the only one falling for Misty."

"Well, you're wrong if you think I am," he said, leading her out of the living room. "Dead wrong." Sane, sensible men did not fall for dingbats. "Now, let's get you home."

Alan walked his mother along the curve of tree-lined street and down the long sweep of her driveway, a hundred yards from his place.

"When you've had a few days to rest up, would you take Dee so I can give Misty a driving lesson?"

"Rest up? Alan, I'm just back from vacation. You bring Deanna to me first thing tomorrow morning, or I'll come and get her myself. We've really missed Deanna, and have gazillion gifts for her."

"You can have her for an hour tomorrow," he said, "but by then, you'll thank me for not letting her stay longer. The driving lessons can wait a few days." He needed time to recover his senses. Clearly, he also needed to date a few more women, if merely touching Misty's thigh through her gown could send him into such a tailspin he didn't even see her leave, or hear her say good-night. As he knew she would have. Misty was unfailingly polite.

"All right," Jan said reluctantly. Alan was glad his mother, her husband and Deanna had formed such a mutual admiration society. It made it easier to ask them to take Deanna off his hands once in a while. And Lord knew how long it would take Misty to learn to drive, considering her aversion to cars.

Why, it might take weeks, but he saw it as his duty to her. She was handicapped, whether she knew it or not, by her lack of driver's license. Yes, several weeks. For the next several weeks, he'd reserve the hours between nine and noon for Misty's driving lessons.

Whether she thought it a good idea or not.

His eyes were drawn almost by instinct to the window behind which Misty presumably slept. Did he see a faint glow through her drapes? Was she lying awake, thinking? Was she thinking about—

He squelched the thought before it formed fully. Misty had gone to bed, tired. She'd be asleep by now. She'd worked hard all day. She needed her rest. She would not be thinking of him. They'd gotten that out of their systems, both of them, the night they ended up necking in the backyard. He closed his eyes and clenched his fists. He'd *almost* gotten it out of his system. There remained, however, just a hint of residual desire. But only when he thought about it too much.

He crossed his bedroom and slid open the patio door as silently as he could, then stood on the deck listening to the distant sound of the ocean booming against the rocks, hearing a ship's whistle shrill in the quiet night air. When that faded, he also heard Zamfir music emanating from Misty's room. It was Zamfir. Or some other artist on panpipes. He laughed without humor. It was not, absolutely not, what the cleaning woman claimed to have seen.

Without his even being aware of having moved, he found himself around the corner on Misty's side of the deck, only a few feet from her door, listening intently. He clutched the back of a chair and let the sweet, haunting music, like thin silver strings touched by the wind, fill his senses. Behind Misty's drapes, the faint light still flickered, the glow of a single candle? Or maybe a shaft of moonlight caught in the folds of the curtains? He glanced at the sky. There was no moon.

Had she gone to sleep with a tape on? Wondering about that, he dropped into the chair and put his feet on the end of the chaise. Did she use a night-light? Was Misty afraid of the dark?

He had to smile, remembering her solemn, apprehensive face as she said, "Elves are brave." Why had the thought of kissing him frightened her? Why had she done it despite that? Because, like him, she could not resist?

His mother was right. Misty was one very intriguing nanny.

THAT WAS ALAN on the deck. Misty covered her ears to hide the creak of wicker as he shifted in his chair, only a few feet from her door. What was he doing? What was he thinking about?

She could have found out quite easily, but refrained; there was no need. Really, being an elf wasn't all good, all the time. Those restrictions could be irritating. Still, what if he were thinking about something she needed to know, such as the woman he might like to have as a wife? If she didn't know what he wanted, how was she supposed to help him? Even his mother agreed he needed a wife.

Gently, she nudged at the gates of his mind, then jerked back.

No. She could not do it. Because what if he was thinking about— She jerked back from even her own thoughts. They, too, were forbidden. By her own edict. Some things were best left entirely alone.

His chair creaked again. Why didn't he go to bed?

Why didn't she?

Curiosity. That was why. That was all.

Well, maybe a bit of remembering those kisses, too. If his mother hadn't showed up, would they have ended up kissing each other again tonight? Though she wasn't cold—indeed, she felt feverish—she shivered and folded her wings around her.

Without giving it much thought, she winked out and perched on the eaves trough above and behind him, feet swinging, ankles crossed.

He liked her feet. She knew that. Each time he looked at them, she felt warm all over, more so since he had touched them that evening when she sat on the slide—the evening he had kissed her. The evening she had kissed him back. Always, her thoughts returned to that, even though thinking about it disturbed her, left her confused. As much as looking at his dark, thick, erotic curls disturbed and confused her.

They gleamed faintly in the glow of a streetlight shining through the trees. She knew now just how nice they felt. Maybe if she touched them, just a little, without his knowing, she'd be satisfied and then be able to sleep.

She fluttered down behind him, silently, stealthily, scarcely more than another shadow in a night filled with them. She hovered over his head, let her toes touch, just a whisper, just brushing the tops of his curls. Ah, but were they ever soft! Almost as silken as the gown she'd made for herself, and as sensuous to the touch.

She dug her feet in a little deeper, feeling his curls coil around her ankles. Suddenly, as if sensing her presence, he moved restlessly, releasing the mingled scents of shampoo, soap and man. Misty's heart fluttered as hard as her wings and she jerked her feet out of Alan's hair.

In a wink, she was back in her room, on the middle of her bed, in a terrible tangle of arms, legs and wings. She turned off the moon and scudding clouds with which she'd decorated her ceiling and quickly resumed human form.

Sitting on her bed with her arms wrapped around herself, she stared into the dark.

Her heart raced. Cold, clammy skin shivered inside the silk of her gown. She changed her garment to the softest of fur and cuddled it close, thinking soothing thoughts.

On the deck, Alan ran a hand through his hair and leaned his head back to gaze at the stars. From out of the night, those silvery strains of music resumed. He turned to glance at Misty's window. The flickering light went out. The music changed, becoming the beguiling babble of water bubbling against pebbles in a stream, the splash of a fountain, the whisper of a breeze. Or of a woman sighing his name.

He sighed, rose and went inside, annoyed with himself for getting fanciful again. For behaving as if he were bewitched.

FRIDAY AFTERNOON, Misty and Deanna arrived home from the library with a stack of books, to find the house empty, almost hollow sounding, though Alan was the only thing missing. A note, propped on the counter, informed them he'd be having dinner with "a friend."

Another popsie? Misty wondered, and tried to put the matter out of her mind, but a desolate sensation invaded her, as if she'd been cast adrift with nothing to anchor her in reality.

Reality?

Misty brought herself up short. Reality was anything she chose to create. If she wanted to conjure up a warm, home-and-hearth atmosphere for herself, then she could. She would. She did not require a man to help her do that. Even if it was his house. It was Deanna's, too, and the child's lovely aura filled it.

Then Deanna went to sleep.

Misty curled up on her mossy couch and kept busy juggling scenery, trying to discover exactly the right blend of sight, sound, sensation and scent to soothe her, to help her rest. If she could have, she'd have winked out and gone home, visited her friends, shot a few games of pool or simply soared for a day or a year on a high-rising thermal, but to leave Deanna for even an instant would have been wrong.

Suddenly, the wounded aura surrounding Alan's house shimmered, warmed, became whole, and Misty sent most of her distractions home, sitting very still and waiting, not breathing, for the sound of his key in the door. Her heart turned cartwheels of joy. He was home much earlier than she'd expected. Maybe he hadn't had dinner, after all? Maybe he'd want her to prepare something for him? Maybe he'd want— No! She didn't want that, either!

Quickly creating her green nanny dress, she forced herself to take the slow way down the stairs.

"Hello," she said, wincing at the red-and-black swirl of his ill humor. "Did you and your popsie have a nice dinner?"

He stared at her, the dark swirl developing a few yellow streaks. His mouth twitched and she felt his amusement begin to tickle. "Not really," he said. "The *lady* developed a 'headache' halfway through, and left." He grinned. "And I don't suppose she'd appreciate being referred to as a 'popsie.'"

"Oh. I'm sorry," she said. "That's how you referred to dates. Is it not the correct word?"

He laughed, and she saw his bad mood fading. "In some cases, yes. In this case, no."

"What is a popsie? How do you tell the difference?"

He looked at her strangely, then shrugged. "A popsie is the kind of woman a man dates when he just wants a good time, a bit of light entertainment and a . . . a dinner companion."

Misty sniffed. That was a euphemism if she'd ever heard one. "Someone to go to bed with, you mean."

A touch of color burned high on his cheekbones, but he answered evenly enough, and honestly, she knew. "Sometimes."

"Not someone who would make a good mother for Deanna, then." She must have known that instinctively. That explained the heavy heart she had all the while when he was out.

He ignored that and repeated his earlier reply. "As I said, sometimes, but not always. And not this time."

She met his gaze. "This one has the potential to become Deanna's new mother?"

He considered. "Potential? No. I don't think so. She developed that headache and left because I happened to mention you and Deanna a couple times. It was very obvious the subject of my daughter bored her."

Misty was glad he had sense enough to realize the headache had been fake. Still, she said as she turned away, "Maybe if you'd offered her chocolate mousse for dessert, she'd have stayed."

He caught her elbow, drawing her back around. "Chocolate mousse? What's that got to do with anything?"

"That's what your kisses make *me* feel like. Like I've just taken my first mouthful of chocolate mousse. Some women find chocolate addictive. If you mean to find one you want to keep, I suggest you try feeding her chocolate."

He grinned. "Instead of kissing her?"

She shrugged. "That, of course, is up to you."

His lazy smile curled around something inside her. "If it were you, which would you prefer?"

"But it's not going to be me," she said, pulling her elbow free. "Therefore, I'll take the chocolate mousse. Will you?"

"Will I what?"

"Have chocolate mousse with me."

He laughed. "Now?" He hesitated for a second, then smiled again. "If you have some ready, then of course I'll share it with you."

She had it ready, sitting on the table in tall, fluted dishes, with little vanilla wafers stuck in each cup like rabbits' ears, and tiny mint leaves to make it look pretty, before they even reached the kitchen door.

DURING THE REST of the evening, Misty discovered a different kind of magic from any she'd ever known. Alan fascinated her with tales about his boyhood, the scrapes he'd gotten into at every new army base his father's career took them to, as he tried to impress other kids and make friends. He brought tears to her eyes when he spoke of being sent to board at a military academy when he was twelve, to "prepare him for following in his father's footsteps."

Her heart ached with the pain he pretended he'd long since forgotten as he related his futile struggle to fit in. Even with that background, the military college training that had followed academy had been a horror show. It paled, though, in comparison to the family scene when he'd simply walked away from college mere weeks before graduation. Misty knew, without his saying, how deeply his father's rage and disapproval had affected him.

"But it was what I wanted to do," he said with a casual shrug, as if it had been a decision lightly made, which she knew it had not. "My choice. I knew how

Dad would react. I sat on my bed, polishing my boots that night, looked around me and saw six other men with identical haircuts to mine, each using identical motions, seated on identical beds, and each with an identical mind-set. Their goal was to look sharp, study hard, graduate in the top ten and be accepted by the regiment of their choice. My goal was to get through.

"I asked myself why I wanted to get through, when getting through wasn't going to get me out of uniform, wasn't going to gain me any freedom, wasn't going to provide me with a future I wanted.

"I set my boots down, stood, put on my cap and walked out the door. Then I kept on walking, out the gate, along the road and into a future of my own choosing."

"It was a brave thing to do, Alan."

He shrugged and fiddled with a spoon, not meeting her gaze. "Not according to my father. He called it cowardice, and called me a disgrace to the family. I was supposed to be the third generation of Magnus men with an outstanding military career." He glanced up. "I'm just sorry I couldn't be the man he wanted me to be."

"But you're the man you wanted you to be," she said. "Isn't that more important?"

After a moment, he nodded. Then, as if it were only the natural progression of things, he told her about his time with Deanna's mother. "In a way, I'm glad my dad didn't live long enough to learn I'd fathered a child and failed to support her through her early years. He thought a man who neglected his family's finances was the lowest of the low. Not knowing wouldn't have been an adequate excuse. A man should make it his business to know, to look after his woman and children."

"What about the other kinds of support, Alan? Didn't he think a man owed his family that, as well?"

She read swift anger and repudiation in his stare, felt it in the crackle of air around him. "Of course he did. He might have spent a lot of time away from us, but he loved us all."

Misty reached across the table to touch his hand. "I wasn't suggesting otherwise. But understanding another's needs is part of caring and supporting, and he had little understanding of yours. Putting you in a military boarding school must have been like trapping jinni in a lamp."

She shuddered. "Such cruelty to blind eyes that see as yours do, and to leave no outlet for your imagination, no room for your creativity to grow. I'm not surprised you walked away eventually."

His laugh was brief and bitter. "Dad was. He felt I'd been living a lie all those years, pretending to conform, pretending to want what he wanted for me. He never seemed to recall the times I told him it wasn't for me. I believe he died still thinking I'd done it all only so I could betray him in the end, shame him in front of his friends and colleagues. He was sure I'd end up living on skid road, that he'd failed in the most basic of a father's tasks, instilling certain values in his children."

He laughed again. "But the odd thing is, I do share his values. I want to make a proper home for Deanna, with all the security I enjoyed growing up, and not just for her, but for myself, as well. That's why I bought this house, rather than a condo. I wanted a sense of permanency. Of course, it was conveniently close to my mother, and she needed me after Dad died."

His face tightened. "He'd been retired for only a year when he was killed in a hunting accident. He'd invited me to fly out and accompany him. He was trying, I know, to get the two of us back on track." Regret tinged his tone. "I refused the invitation."

"You think if you had been with him it wouldn't have happened?"

"No. No, I don't think that. He was a firearms expert, knew what he was doing. It was the kid who mistook him for a moose who didn't know."

"You dislike hunting."

His sharp glance reminded her that she should have phrased it as a question. "That's not the point, and it wasn't why I refused to come. I knew then it wasn't hunting he was offering, but time for us to be alone together, to maybe reach an understanding of each other's lives."

"Bonding."

"Yeah. That's what they call it. But I was too busy, too caught up in a story I was working on. I let an imaginary world blind me to my father's very real need to make amends."

"You didn't know he was going to die."

"Nor did I know he wasn't." She could see he was determined to continue blaming himself.

"You know," Alan went on, "I wish I'd had a chance to tell him that what he gave me, growing up, is the kind of life I want for my children. The kind he and Mom gave Melissa and me, despite the constant moves, despite the military discipline."

Misty nodded. "It's the life every child deserves, and too few can have. We'll get it for Deanna, Alan. And for you. Now that you've started seeing ladies, you'll need to bring them home so I can get to work on them."

She sighed as she shoved back her chair and got to her feet. "As much as I'd like to be, even an elf can't be in two places at once, and Deanna's care is my first priority."

At the door of her room Alan stroked her cheek with one finger, as if he were brushing away a lock of hair. Or a tear.

"Misty, wouldn't you rather be a real woman, than an elf?"

She searched his eyes. "I don't know, Alan. I've never been a real woman. I don't know what it feels like."

"I think you do," he said, curling a lock of her hair around his finger and using that to draw her closer to him. She obeyed the gentle urging, unable to do otherwise. "I think this makes you feel like one."

He bent and brushed his lips over hers. Without her intending it to happen, hers parted. Her arms stole around his neck as she pressed close to him. Her heart pounded as a real woman's would. Her breasts swelled against his chest and her knees trembled. She didn't know if a real woman would be that weak, but it didn't matter; Alan was there to hold her up.

The taste of him filled her. His scent made her dizzy. The sound of his ragged breath as he broke the kiss but continued to hold her left her in no doubt that he, a real man, responded to her exactly as he would if she were a real woman.

"Alan . . ." She lifted her head from its nest in the crook of his shoulder. "Your kisses make me want you very much."

He swallowed visibly. "But?"

"I didn't say but."

"Oh, I think you did, Misty." He kissed her again, hard, but briefly. "Now, please. Go into your room and lock your door."

"Lock it?"

"Yes. Because..." He stepped back from her. "Just do it, okay?"

"Alan? Don't I please you? Most men find elves very pleasing."

He lifted his hand and drew that same bent finger over the curve of her cheek again. "You please me, Misty. You please me so much I think you've made it impossible for me to settle for a—" He grinned. "For a popsie ever again. But..." He hesitated, took another step away from her and then continued.

"But I want a woman who doesn't pretend to be an elf, one who is content with what she is, who she is, because then I can be pretty sure she'll be content with who and what I am."

She wanted to cry. "I'm not pretending anything, Alan."

He put a hand on his doorknob. "If you say so." Then, after another moment's pause, he said, "Mom's going to take care of Deanna tomorrow. You're having your first driving lesson."

She opened her mouth to protest, but he shook his head. "Now don't worry about it. You'll do fine. But wear something easy to drive in. Maybe your jeans and some flat, comfortable shoes."

"Comfortable shoes?" Even an elf knew an oxymoron when she heard one. And as for the jeans, she hadn't worn them since her first evening in his house. He had reacted to them too strongly, though he hadn't said a word. He'd liked them, she knew, but disliked liking them.

"I don't have those jeans anymore."

His tone blended amusement and impatience. "Well, wear a different pair, then. We'll leave right after breakfast."

She sighed. "Alan—"

"Hey," he interrupted. "Didn't you tell me that elves are very brave, that they have to be because they get into all sorts of dangerous situations? Consider this just one more of those, Misty. And trust me. You'll do fine."

IT APPALLED MISTY how hard her heart pounded as she readied herself in the morning. Not quite as hard as when Alan was kissing her, but close. She had to force herself to breathe evenly, deeply, calmly. It took several minutes, but she finally managed it. Then, with hardly any effort at all, she winked on some jeans and a sweatshirt, and then stood staring down at her feet, wondering what to do about "comfortable" shoes.

To her surprise, as she thought about it, her feet were suddenly shod, though through no act of her own. She stared at the white deerskin moccasins with blue, red and green beading decorating the toes. Their long, fringed tongues folded over and flipped prettily when she took an experimental step. They felt nice. The were kind to her feet, almost as kind as no shoes at all.

See? said a voice in her head. *Nothing's impossible when you want it badly enough.*

Mother! She recognized the source of both voice and moccasins with no difficulty at all. In the mirrored closet doors, she saw a faint shimmer of light, a halo of silver around a swirl of green. "Your interference is making my whole life impossible!" she said. "I need to come home and discuss this matter with you, but you're making *that* impossible, too! I want to know why!"

The shimmering light flickered, and then was gone, leaving only an echo in Misty's mind of the words she hadn't really heard, but had understood nevertheless: *Nothing's impossible if you want it badly enough.*

She sat on the side of her bed, staring at her moccasins. Did that mean if she wanted badly enough to go home, not even the Mother's machinations could prevent it? Well, she knew that, of course. If she really wanted to go home, she could do so merely by asking Deanna to release her. But she didn't want to leave permanently. She wanted nothing more than a chance to discuss it, to seek advice on how to handle all that was happening to her emotions.

Was the Mother saying she believed Misty didn't truly want what she claimed to want? Why wouldn't she discuss it with her?

Of course, if she did go home for a face-to-face confrontation, she'd have to admit that she'd found herself in yet another situation where she couldn't cope. She didn't want to do that, didn't want to say again, "Mother, I've failed in my task."

I will not fail this time. I can do it. I am an elf. I can do anything.

She was still muttering the same affirmations as Alan returned from having taken Deanna to his mother. "Ready?" he said, as if there had never been a moment's doubt in his mind that she'd comply with his wishes.

"Yes," she said, doubts and fears toying with her nerves, but his smile, and the hand he held out toward her, lifted her spirits while it addled her senses.

"Come on, Misty," he said, towing her through the door into the garage. "This is going to be fun."

She wished she could control the small, independent bit of her heart that agreed.

IT WASN'T MUCH FUN at first. It took her at least an hour to get used to being in the car with him and his disturbing, distracting scent. The place he took her for the lesson was quiet, though, with no other cars to worry about, and she only went off the road twice, when she breathed too deeply and got dizzy.

The second time, he had to get behind the wheel and drive the car out of the ditch, but he did it in such an easygoing manner, she began to relax. She relaxed even more when the morning grew warmer and they opened all the windows so his scent didn't interfere with her concentration quite so strongly.

After that, it became easier. When she saw the ditch coming at her, she moved it. Presently, she learned that she could move the car instead, by turning the wheel just so, and Alan didn't gasp and clutch at the dashboard quite so often.

The road he'd chosen was far out in the country, and bumpy, with too many holes. The back of the station wagon bounced and rattled each time they hit one. Alan said it was an abandoned logging road. She could see why they'd abandoned it. It was a mess. She'd like to try threading the car in and out between other vehicles, as Alan did, and following a yellow line on one side, and a white line on the other. It would surely be an improvement over this.

"When do I get to drive on a real road with other drivers?"

"Maybe in a couple of years," he said, biting his lip as she straightened another tight curve to make it easier to navigate.

"Oh." She looked at him. "I didn't think it would take that long. Two years is quite a long time on Earth, isn't it? Why, Deanna will be in school in two years and she won't need me."

"Watch the road!" he shouted. She glanced forward to see a stump coming toward them, and moved it.

"Dammit, Misty," he said, breathing hard, "maybe Deanna will be in school in two years, but she'll still need *me* for a good many years to come so I'd appreciate it if you'd slow down until you have a bit more control."

Obediently, she slowed down.

Ten minutes later, he said, speaking between his teeth, "You can go a *little* faster than this."

Happily, she obliged and Alan appeared to relax, letting her drive on for another hour or so, up and down the same stretch of road. Then, taking the wheel, he drove them down a long hill to a road with lines on it, and more cars. Presently, they reached a small town where they stopped and had lunch.

He grinned at her over the menu. "Darn. No chocolate mousse. Does that mean I have to kiss you?"

"No!" She sat back on her side of the booth lest he lean across the table and do as he suggested. She knew she couldn't drive another foot if he kissed her. If he did, she wouldn't be able to drive for days and days, until her soul calmed down.

And she did like driving.

Maybe not as much as she'd liked kissing Alan, but she knew what was good for her and what was not. Driving was at least a skill she might use on other assignments. If she kissed Alan too many times, there might not *be* any more assignments. It was a sobering thought.

"You don't have to be so adamant about it," he said, slapping the menu onto the table. "I was kidding when I said that. I have no intention of kissing you."

She nodded, feeling more than just a little disappointed. "I understand." But if she were able to lie, if she could tell him she *didn't* believe she was an elf, then would he?

Once back in the car, he said, "I think you're ready for a real road. Hop in."

It was the last coherent thing he said for a long time.

9

"WHEE!" MISTY CRESTED a hill, saw an elderly man pushing a rusty shopping cart full of cans and other urban detritus and, with a wave of her right index finger, deposited him, his cart and his beer cans safely on the other side of the road. The car swept on, zooming down the back side of the hill, tires squealing as she negotiated a corner without straightening it out for her own convenience.

Using the steering wheel was a real art, she'd discovered, and she enjoyed being artful.

Hills, she'd quickly learned, were wonderful fun, too, especially on a smooth road where she could go really fast.

"Whee!" she cried again as they nearly took off at the top. "Oh, Alan, you were right! This is great! I wish I had learned to drive centuries ago!"

Alan, his hands splayed on the dashboard, his feet planted on the floor, spoke through lips pulled tight over his teeth.

"Misty. Stop. The. Car." It was the third time he'd said it in as many minutes but she knew he didn't mean it. It would be irrational of him to want her to stop. How could he teach her to drive if the car wasn't going anywhere? That, after all, was the priority. She needed to have a driver's license so she could take Deanna places. If she didn't do that, she'd be neglecting her duties. It was a bonus that this particular duty had turned out to be such a delight.

"You don't mean that." She looked at him. "I'm doing fine, aren't I? Have I hit anything yet? Have I gone in the ditch since way before lunch?"

He said nothing, only pointed ahead, making a croaking sound. The back end of a school bus loomed broad and blunt, and Misty winked it out of the way, then glanced in the mirror to see it safely trundling along the road behind them.

"There, see? No harm done," she said, looking at Alan again. To her amazement, he had slumped forward as far as his seat belt would permit, his arms hanging limp, hands dangling, head flopped forward.

She sent out a gentle probe and discovered he was unconscious.

She stopped the car. Abruptly.

His seat belt snapped him upright, pinned him against the seat back and his eyes popped open. So did his mouth at the sound of screaming tires behind them. As he wrenched himself around to cast a horrified stare out the back window, Misty took another glance in the mirror, saw the same school bus weaving as its driver fought for control and winked it out of the way again. This time, she set it down in front of her car, perfectly safe, though it continued to weave for a second or two until she sent soothing thoughts toward its driver.

Poor man. He must be as hysterically inclined as Alan.

For a man who'd said he was calm and cool and never panicked in emergencies, Alan certainly had done a lot of panicking today. Not that there had ever been a real emergency, either—just what he considered emergencies until she fixed whatever little mistake she'd made.

"Really," she said, "I'm just a beginner, Alan. I'd have thought you'd expect me to make mistakes."

He gurgled.

"May I start the car again?"

She thought his throaty moan was assent, but as she moved her foot to place it on the gas, he grabbed her knee and dragged it upward so she could do nothing but wiggle her ankle ineffectually, making the fringes on her moccasin dance and the beads flash color.

"What are you doing?" she demanded. His touch sent a shiver through her. It took every ounce of her self-control to withstand the assault on her senses as she, too, took a deep breath, smelling him. "The logging road would have been a better choice, Alan, if this is when we get to molest each other."

He let her knee go so abruptly her foot fell to the floor. With another inarticulate gurgle, he twisted the key in the ignition and pulled it out. Then he stuffed it deep into his pocket and leaned his head back against the rest. For several minutes, he breathed deeply, steadily, as Misty sat there watching him.

Without looking at her, he lifted his head, opened the door and tried to alight. His seat belt made it impossible. With a muttered curse, he reached for the clasp, but she thought it undone for him and he stared at her, then staggered out.

At the front of the car, he placed his hands on the hood, looking in at her through the windshield for a long, long time. Several vehicles passed them, two of them with long, angry blares of the horn.

Then, walking a little more steadily, Alan came around to the driver's door, opened it and said in a soft, expressionless voice, "Move over."

"Over where?"

"To the passenger side."

Disappointed, she continued to clutch the steering wheel as she gazed up at him. "Is my driving lesson over?"

He nodded. "Over." He shuddered. "Yes."

"Can we do it again tomorrow?"

"No. Your driving lessons are over. Permanently."

"Oh, good. I learned fast, didn't I? You were right. It was fun! I thought there'd be no *whee* in driving a car, but there really is, Alan. Thank you for teaching me." She reached up, slipped a hand behind his head, pulled him down and kissed him square on the lips. He'd only said he wasn't going to kiss her. She hadn't said any such thing about him. She wished she'd thought of it from that angle earlier.

It was wonderful! There was a lot of *whee* in kissing Alan, too. After a moment, he got right into the kiss with her, crouching to make it easier, wrapped one hand around her back, the other on an arm. He pulled her out of the seat.

Standing, he kept her cradled against his chest, leaned on the side of the car and pulled her between his legs. His mouth moved over hers, soft, then hard, seeking, then offering.

Misty's heart sang, her breasts swelled, her nipples peaked and dizziness overcame her so that she had to cling to Alan to remain on her feet.

A horn blared, startling them, breaking them apart. A truck driver hollered, "Go park, you idiot!"

Alan groaned and slowly slid his hands off Misty's backside.

"I guess he's right. This isn't the time or the place."

Misty slipped over to the passenger side where she leaned back in the place where he'd been sitting, feeling remnants of his aura still there, drawing in his dizzying scent. "Do I get my proper driving test now?"

He groaned again and laid his hand over his eyes. "I did not teach you anything," he said. "This lesson never happened. I'm having a nightmare, and when I wake up I will remember it in each, livid, horrifying detail, and then I will tell you that I will never give you a driving lesson, that no one on this earth will ever give you one if I'm alive to hear about it, and I will lock up the car keys in a place where you can never get at them."

"There is no such place, Alan," she said with a laugh. "But if you tell me not to touch them, then of course I won't. Not yours."

He put the key in the ignition, his trembling hand making the others hanging down rattle like jingle bells. "I'm telling you. You will never touch a car key again." His fists tight around the wheel, he looked at her for the first time since they'd gotten back into the car. "Never, Misty. Never ever again. Got it?"

She returned his solemn gaze, puzzled. "Got it."

Neither said another word until they pulled up in front of his mother's house. Jan, who was cutting back spent flower heads, stood erect, rubbing her back, and smiled at the both of them as Deanna came tearing across the lawn to fling herself into her father's arms.

"How did the driving lesson go?" Jan asked, removing her gardening gloves.

"Oh, it was wonderful!" Misty replied. "But Alan fainted."

"Isn't that amazing," said Jan. "His father did that, too, when he tried to teach me."

She patted her son's cheek. "Never mind, dear. I'll teach Misty."

Misty had real concern that he might faint again, but before he did, his mother continued, "Now I think you and Misty should go home, get all gussied up and go out for dinner to celebrate her first driving lesson. Deanna wants to spend the night with us."

Misty, halfway across the lawn with Deanna, came to an abrupt halt.

"All night?" her voice squeaked, and Alan's swift, suddenly hot glance reminded her too well of those kisses they'd shared before the truck driver yelled at them. What had Alan said? That it wasn't the time or the place?

With only the two of them at home, she knew as well as she knew anything, there'd be nothing to act as even a psychological barrier.

She didn't breathe, waiting for Alan to reply to his mother's suggestion.

Out of a long silence, his voice came to her. "Misty?"

Slowly, she turned around and faced him. He'd nearly caught up with her. Looking down at her, he seemed to be searching her eyes. "Would you like that?"

"Dinner?" she said faintly.

He nodded, his gaze locked with hers. "Remember? We did discuss it last week. We just never got around to it. But tonight we have a baby-sitter."

"I know." Dimly, she remembered Deanna wanted to show her something. Just as dimly, she sensed Alan's mother watching them. Jan kept her distance, but Misty knew she was completely aware of the coiled energy between her son and the nanny. It was as if everyone around the two of them held their collective breaths, even the breeze in the shrubbery, the birds in the trees.

Misty couldn't speak. She could scarcely think. She feared for a moment she'd turn back into elf form, terrifying Alan's mother and giving his stepfather, who was strolling toward them, heart failure. It took all her strength to maintain her present shape.

Alan watched a series of emotions cross Misty's face. Why didn't she say something? He'd asked her to have dinner with him. She looked as if he'd proposed something indecent.

Or proposed marriage.

He drew a deep breath and let it out slowly, willing her to reply. "Misty?" he said finally into her taut silence.

As he watched her mull it over, he knew suddenly that to her his invitation had greater import than he'd realized. He was proposing, not something indecent, not necessarily marriage just yet, not necessarily that ever, but something requiring a commitment on her part. And on his.

Until that moment, he hadn't realized how great a commitment he was willing to make, or how much of one he wanted her to offer.

But she had known it. She had known it from his original mention of a dinner date, he now realized, from the first assumption that he had to be the one to give her driving lessons, from before their first kiss. She had known that if they were alone together for any length of time, the outcome would be inevitable. Had they been together enough? Too much? Especially following so close upon the emotionally charged aftermath to her scaring him almost witless?

Almost? He removed the qualifier. She had scared him witless. So witless he'd kissed her until neither of them could think straight. Was he, again, rushing things? Rushing her?

Maybe, but he sensed in her an equal urgency, and recognized his own inability to slow the pace of this relationship. It was out of control. Besides, she'd kissed him first today.

Tension spiraled between them, and escalated. He held his breath, and waited.

If she refused dinner with him tonight, he'd know she was refusing much more than that. He'd know she wasn't ready for the next step. And he was. He wanted to touch her, wanted to persuade her with his kisses, with his need, with the need he knew he could engender in her, but seduction wasn't his aim.

Then what was?

He didn't think he could name it yet, but he wanted more. How much more, he couldn't have said. How much more, he was afraid to contemplate.

But he knew that whatever started over dinner tonight would take them farther than he had ever gone before.

Misty knew the right answer to give Alan. She knew the penalties for giving the wrong one. Could she face them? Could she be what he needed her to be? What he believed her to be? Could she live the life she knew could result if she failed to convince him she was what she claimed to be?

No! No! The answer came instinctively, as it always had in other such circumstances when she'd been forced to ask it. She was an elf. She liked being an elf. She wanted never to be anything *but* an elf. But despite its immediacy, the response lacked conviction because she wanted Alan, too, in every way there was for a woman to want a man, or for an elf to want a mortal.

She wanted both.

A dragonfly whizzed. *Have your cake and eat it, too?* said a voice in her ear.

"Yes," Misty said, then again, fiercely, *"Yes!"*

"Good," Alan replied, and she realized he thought she'd been speaking to him. She met his gaze. Could she now say no? Could she ever say no? To him? To all that he asked? To all that she, too, wanted?

Six days, she pleaded silently. *Give me six more days. Let me try to persuade him.*

High in a tree, a blue jay laughed mockingly, saying, "Try! Try! Try!" and Misty knew the Mother believed that whatever she tried, she'd fail. But she also knew she had her six days.

And six nights.

"Yes," she said again. "Dinner sounds fine, Alan." She paused a beat. "And dancing?"

He nodded, a muscle in his jaw bunching spasmodically. "Wine and candlelight, Misty." She also heard the words he did not speak aloud: *Everything, I'm offering you everything. And asking for everything in return.* His voice deepened as he continued. "Chocolate mousse for dessert."

She closed her eyes, doubts and fears and hopes and dreams a confused welter behind her lids, but the urgency growing within her won out.

Six days? She knew how resistant he was, knew that deep inside he had already recognized the truth about her, but remained unwilling—perhaps even unable—to admit it to himself. Somehow, she was going to have to find a way to make a believer out of this disbelieving man.

She opened her eyes and looked at him, then at Deanna, who, as if sensing the significance of the negotiations between her father and her elf, had remained silent during the exchange.

The reasons for staying, regardless, loomed higher and higher in Misty's heart. It wasn't just Alan. It wasn't just herself she needed to consider. There was Deanna. Her trust, her love, both so freely given, along with her willing acceptance, and her need.

"Yes," Misty said on a long sigh, knowing what her agreement meant, where it would lead. "Chocolate mousse, too."

DANCING WITH ALAN was as discombobulating as being in the car with him, but not as disturbing as kissing him. Ever since the waiter had come and asked if they'd care for dessert, and Alan had met her gaze while he said, "No, we'll take care of that ourselves, at home," she'd wanted to be at home with him.

She'd said so, but he'd smiled and drawn her to the small dance floor. "Let's not rush this, Misty. We have all evening. All night." He'd paused for a moment, then added, pulling her close, speaking against her ear, "All the rest of our lives."

All the rest of our lives . . . or six days. She held back the words, held back the fear, held back the pain, reminding herself that elves were brave. Even if in making this choice, she must cease to enjoy the powers of an elf, she could still be brave.

To choose the alternative would surely require more courage.

Dancing became a delicious torture, one Misty could take for only so long. Presently, lifting her head from his shoulder, kissing him under the chin, she said, "Alan, let's go home now."

His smile stole her breath. "Yes."

Misty could have gotten them there much faster, but she let Alan do it his way. After all, it was his ways she might need to become accustomed to. The more she breathed his scent, the more right that choice seemed. Even if she couldn't convince him. She could adapt.

ALAN'S BLOOD SIMMERED hotter even than when Misty had agreed to dinner, dancing and "chocolate mousse." Prolonging the agony had been just that, but it was a kind of agony he welcomed. With Misty across from him dressed in a simple sheath of a deep, rich purple that reflected in her eyes, he could have dined on air and felt satisfied. He wanted Misty to have the whole thing, though—the elegant waiters, the bubbling champagne, the superbly presented meal. The courtship.

If this was to be her courtship, though it might be short, he wanted it to be memorable for her.

Still, hadn't he been courting her without knowing it from the moment he saw her in the yard with Deanna? So short a time, and so filled with moments he wanted to savor, to cherish. As he wanted to savor this evening, make it last.

But her whispered plea that he take her home had brought his tenuous control to very near its limits.

Now, as he unlocked the door, he wondered if he'd even get upstairs before he took what he needed.

As he turned on the hall light, Misty smiled at him and took two steps away. He caught the ends of the light wrap she wore around her shoulders and used it to propel her toward him. "Don't rush away," he said. "Unless you've changed your mind."

He searched her eyes for any signs of hesitation, remembering how quiet she had been in the car, and the stillness of her hand as he held it with his on the steering wheel. But he saw no reluctance in those purple depths.

"I haven't changed my mind."

"Up to a certain point," he said, his voice ragged, "you can, you know. But, Misty, please understand this, there is that point. If you don't want this, you need to tell me now."

"I want this," she whispered. "I want you." She swayed toward him, tilted her face, linked her hands behind his head and pulled him down to her.

Alan lost himself in her.

Moments later, he stared at her in awe. "I think," he managed to say, "I'm beginning to believe in magic. At least your brand of it."

She smiled. "Good. I want you to."

She slipped out of his arms and took a step toward the stairs. As if she had him on a string the way she did Deanna's toy dog, he pursued her. She trailed her scarf behind her like a lure, trailed her scent, trailed a lingering glance over her shoulder, and a smile that drew him on.

Willingly, helpless, he followed.

As they entered her sitting room, light flooded it from a source Alan could not see. Filtered sunlight? At eleven in the evening? No! His mind rejected the idea even as his body felt the warmth of that sun.

He blinked. He gaped at the low, green couch that nestled against the two walls forming a corner of the room. It looked for all the world as if it were made of oss. He smelled the musky, woodsy scent of it and the immer in his blood rose toward a boil.

A bright flash of gold, a sparkling shower of water drops and the sounds of their splattering jerked his gaze to a circle of wet rocks surrounding a bubbling spring embedded in the floor. Again, a goldfish jumped, splashing more water onto the rocks.

No! He was hallucinating. Either that, or Misty had hypnotized him. Had there been some funny mushrooms in the sauce? Was he suffering from some kind of neurological disorder? He felt fine, maybe a touch too warm, but the sun could account for that and—

There was no sun, dammit!

Hypnosis couldn't account, though, for his following Misty as she continued on her way across the plush—oh, God!—*plush grass* that covered the floor, and into her bedroom.

"Misty..." His voice croaked out. Over her bed hung a bower of blossoms. There were birds twittering and butterflies fluttering. "Misty, what have you done in here? What are you doing to *me?*"

"What do you want me to do to you?"

Her purple sheath shimmered and pooled at her feet. Misty stood naked before him but for the tiniest pair of bikini panties he had ever seen. Her erect nipples, bright pink and perfectly centered in her perfectly formed breasts, pointed straight at him.

He didn't move. He knew he hadn't moved. But suddenly he, too, was naked. He swayed, but Misty was there to slide her arms around him.

He clung to her, buried his face in her hair. If he had some terrible disease and was going to die of it, he wanted *this,* before. He wanted Misty, regardless of what his good sense told him, regardless of the jibbering idiot in the back of his brain that told him his eyes couldn't deceive him. He knew they could, knew they had; his eyes, his ears, his nose, they'd all deceived and betrayed him, but his other senses, touch, taste, feasted on Misty, yet increased his hunger to the point of madness.

It was a madness he could no longer deny.

The heat of her burned in his belly, fired his need, stoked it higher and higher as she demanded his mouth on hers, bit his lower lip, stroked it with her darting tongue, then nibbled him again. He squeezed his eyes shut to block out the sights he knew he wasn't really seeing anyway, let her perfume override the other scents he knew he could not truly smell, and took command of the kiss.

He mastered her, mastered his own raging desire, tamed it for the moment. Control. He needed control. He needed to slow down and give her all the varied pleasure she deserved.

Oh, God, she tasted so sweet. He plundered her mouth again, and when she whimpered her pleasure, the sound of that drove him closer to the edge. He eased off—and she took the lead.

She bewitched him. She tormented him. She drew him along a path that could have only one end, and had that end meant diving off a cliff into boiling breakers, he'd have followed her as willingly as he'd trailed her up the stairs. In the end, though, it was she who gasped and broke their kiss. She laid her head on his shoulder, her chest heaving as she dragged in ragged breaths, her heart hammering so hard he felt it against his ribs. He stroked her hair with his cheek, his hands sliding over her back, thinking of anything he thought would cool his burn.

Presently, it eased off to the level of a roaring blast furnace, contained but by no means extinguished.

And not for long.

She smoothed her hands over his heaving shoulders, as if trying to soothe a wild beast, and like a wild beast, he trembled under her caresses.

With a growl, he shrugged her nestled cheek off his shoulder and commanded her mouth again, kissing her deeply, thoroughly, trying to fill himself with the taste of her, the feel, the scent. Her breasts seemed almost to singe him as he moved her against his chest, sideways, back and forth, then gently up and down. She gasped as she tore her mouth from his and flung her head back, her body taut as a bow. He kissed her throat, pressing his mouth against the rapidity of her pulse, drinking in the tang of her skin. She dug her nails into his back and he nipped at her shoulders, the taut cords of her neck, nuzzled the soft skin under her ears, until he thought he couldn't stand anymore.

"Please," she whispered. "Oh, please..."

He lifted her, laid her on the bed, lying beside her, feeling as if he lay on a cloud. Slowly, slowly, he drew her wispy panties down over her hips, her thighs, her knees. Overhead, the birds grew silent, the butterflies still, but the perfume of the flowers remained, and the perfume of the woman, to set his senses areel.

He loved her shudders, loved her whispers, loved the shape of her, but most of all he loved the pinkness of her feet through the lace of her panties as he pulled the garment off. He loved her neat toes, her slender ankles. He kissed each toe, pressed her soles against his cheeks, then kissed his way up the inside of her leg.

Misty cried out and reached down as she sat up, drawing Alan up her body, needing his mouth on hers, his heat to cover her. He nudged her hair away with his mouth, then nibbled all around the edges of her ears as if they were the most delicate morsels. He outlined them with the tip of his tongue, breathed softly into them and told her how pretty he thought they were, as pretty as her feet, as pretty as her teeth, as pretty as her breasts.

She laughed in delight, and he stroked his lips over her cheeks, the corners of her mouth. She felt his smile, traced it with the tip of her tongue, and he kissed her eyelids. He trailed kisses down her throat as she straddled his lap, and then, tilting her backward, he took her breast in his mouth.

She moaned as her nipple popped hard against his tongue, Alan's pleased murmur her reward, along with his hands clenching spasmodically on her bottom. She knew her taste pleasured him, and loved knowing it. He drew the bead of her nipple tightly against the roof of his mouth, pressing it there with his tongue, sucking while she held his head to her. She curled her body around him, nestled her cheek against the top of his head, her fingers following the lines of his jaw, stroking him, encouraging him.

Her hand splayed over his shoulder, smoothed across his back. When he shifted his grip under her to free one hand, lifting it to her other breast, she gasped with the sharp need his touch engendered, and raked him with her nails.

He convulsed, thrusting his hips up in response. He lay back, pulling her with him, and rolled until she was beneath him, locked in the cradle she formed for him with her parted legs.

He clutched her tighter. Misty's control slipped faster than she had ever thought it could. While she still had at least a vestige of it, she opened her eyes and looked deep into his. As she gazed at him, she accepted him, accepted the inevitability of what this liaison would mean, and took him into not only her body but her heart.

The world exploded around them. The Mother gave them shooting stars, an aurora like no other and a galaxy of joy.

But as the stars faded and the aurora waned, the joy diminished not one whit.

"I love you," Alan whispered.

I love you, her heart replied, but she pretended not to hear and kissed him in thanks for his words.

They rested, and then her body showed him how her heart felt; her whispers of pleasure told him even more, but throughout the night of loving, never once did Alan hear the words Misty dared not speak. Not even in her mind, lest they be heard in the wrong quarter. Not until she had succeeded in making Alan see the truth.

10

MISTY OPENED HER EYES and saw Alan lying beside her, watching her. His breath caressed her, as did his hand, sweeping down the curve of her waist to shove the sheet back.

"You are so beautiful," he whispered, "you make me want to cry. I adore you, Misty."

It seemed so right, to wake with him beside her, to turn into his embrace, to accept the caresses he gave, the kisses, the heady sensation of loving him. It filled her soul to the brim, spilled over and left her shattered but fulfilled.

They slept again, tangled together, and when Misty awoke the next time, morning sun poured through the sheer drapes. She remembered the vision she had seen the first day, recognized it, acknowledged it with a smile, acknowledged the Mother's wisdom. She gave thanks.

"Hungry?" Alan said against her neck.

"Yes." In truth, she was starved. Remembering the other vision she had seen, the table on the deck, set for two, the single yellow rosebud, the steaming coffee and glistening orange wedges, she smiled and closed her eyes for a second.

"Breakfast," she said, "is served."

"What?"

She blinked hard, but she and Alan still lay on the bed, feet trapped in the tangled sheets. They had not been transported to the deck. No breakfast for two awaited them.

There was no magic.

She stared at him in dismay, and tried again.

"Misty? Sweetheart, what's wrong?"

Oh, Mother! I never said it! I didn't!

But you felt it, child. You do feel it.

No, no, no! But no matter how vehement Misty's denial, the Mother did not relent, did not return her powers. She had fallen in love with a mortal man who would not believe. She was doomed to spend a mortal life on Earth, with nothing but that love to guide her through the maze of mortal living, mortal perils.

She covered her face with her hands.

Alan knelt over her on the bed. "Misty, you're crying. What's wrong?"

Oh, God, had he hurt her? Done something she hated? He pulled her hands down, wiped her tears with the corner of the sheet, but still they fell from her tight-shut eyes.

"Sweetheart, tell me," he said, lifting her against his chest, rocking her from side to side. "Whatever it is, I'll try to make it right. Misty, I love you. Don't cry."

"Oh, Alan," she wept. "I can't make breakfast for you!"

He set her back from him, staring at her. "Is that all? You're crying because I wore you out and you're too tired to move? I didn't expect you to make breakfast for me. I'll make breakfast for you." He laid her back down, pulled the sheet up to her chin and bent to kiss her mouth.

"Rest, my love," he said against her cheek, and she felt his whiskers rasping on her tender skin. No wonder she'd cried. He was a brute, and insensitive, thoughtless. "I'll feed you and make you strong again." He raised his head and smiled. "And when you're strong again, guess what?"

Her smile was as misty as she was, but behind it he saw a rainbow of hope. "What?"

He nuzzled her neck. "Then I'm going to make you weak all over again." She shivered delicately, and he nearly forgot the need to provide for her more prosaic hungers. While he still could, he left her there, made one quick stop in his own room for a bathrobe, then rocketed down the stairs.

Five minutes later, he was back in her room, frowning.

"Misty, there's not a vestige of food in the house."

Her lower lip trembled.

"Hey, it's okay," he said. "I wasn't blaming you. I know I haven't even given a moment's thought to taking you shopping for provisions. It's my fault. I can scarcely believe the incredible meals you've managed despite my forgetfulness."

"Alan—"

He cut her off, sure she was about to insist on shouldering the blame that was rightfully his. "Get dressed, angel face. I'll shower and shave, then we'll go out for breakfast." He grinned. "If we look hard, we may find a place that will serve us chocolate mousse."

He left, and Misty sat on the side of the bed, rocked by total despair.

How could she possibly go out for breakfast?

She truly did not have a thing to wear.

"WHY AREN'T YOU dressed?"

Alan returned to find Misty, still damp from her shower, wrapped in a towel, perched on the edge of the small sofa in her sitting room. For the first time, he remembered his weird vision of the previous night, a couch made of moss, a goldfish pond in the floor, a carpet of grass. Boy! That one took the cake. Of course, it all came back to that strange cleaning lady. He could just count himself lucky, he supposed, that he hadn't seen a little pipe-playing naked man with cloven hooves.

Or if he had, the memory had been wiped out by the sight of a certain naked woman with perfect breasts.

"Misty?"

She lifted tragic eyes to meet his gaze. "I can't get dressed. I have no clothes."

"Of course you have clothes. If you mean you don't have anything suitable for day wear that doesn't look like it belongs to your maiden aunt, then don't worry about it. I'll take you for breakfast no matter what you're wearing. Besides, your jeans are just fine wherever we might go. You, Misty Fawkes, make jeans look like mink."

He turned to her closet, slid open the sliding mirrored doors, stepped in, glanced in disbelief at the empty hangers, opened every drawer and closed it again noisily. All he found in her closet was a pair of white moccasins with blue, red and green beading all across the toes.

"Holy mackerel!" he yelled, backing out, wheeling around to stare at Misty. "Oh, sweetheart! No wonder you're upset! I can't believe they could do that, break in and take everything you own with us sleeping right here."

He joined her on the couch, held her close and stroked her hair. "Don't worry, love. We'll replace everything. I'll call the police, call the insurance company, and— My God! The food! They must have taken the food, too. Jeez! What have we got, some deranged hungry person holed up somewhere in the neighborhood? One with a women's clothing fetish? Or maybe it's a prison escapee who stole clothes and grub because she's hiding out? I'm only glad Deanna wasn't here. I—"

He shot to his feet and grabbed the phone, punching in a number with a suddenly shaking finger. His stepfather answered on the second ring. In the background, he could hear the television blaring, Deanna laughing and his mother saying, "Quiet, lovey, Grandpa's on the phone."

His knees caved in and he sat down hard.

"Hi, Chris," he said, fighting to quell the adrenaline that still insisted he ensure his daughter's safety. He knew she was safe. He could hear her, though her and the TV's volume had both been lowered.

So why had he lunged at the phone and called? He needed to come up with an explanation, and fast, or he'd look like the idiot he was.

"If Dee's okay with you guys for a while longer," he said quickly, "I'm going to take Misty out for breakfast, and then to do some shopping."

Moments later, he hung up and turned to Misty, who posed before the closet doors, draping the large yellow towel this way and that, pinching it closed here, leaving an alarming and delightful length of leg bare there. On her feet, she wore the moccasins.

"You wouldn't," he said.

She looked at him, her eyes large and solemn and filled with defeat he knew she tried hard to hide from him with her insouciant smile. "I would. I will. I am."

He saw her throat work as her smile faltered. "Or do you have a better suggestion?"

"My mother could—" He shook his head. His mother was eight inches taller than Misty and fifty pounds heavier. She'd do as well in *his* clothes.

"Got it," he said. "The skater look. You'll carry that off as well as you do everything else."

Grabbing her hand, he dragged her out into the hall and into his room. There, he flung a pair of jogging shorts on his bed for her, a T-shirt he found tight and an elastic belt to hold the shorts up. "There. Try those on for size," he ordered, and watched with amazement the way she fumbled even such a simple task as donning a T-shirt.

He helped her untangle one arm from the head hole and her head from a sleeve, and in doing so, made them very, very late for breakfast. But when they were finally ready to leave, he breathed a sigh of relief.

Misty's haunted expression was gone, replaced by a satisfied smile and a pretty pink glow in her cheeks. She didn't look ridiculous in his shorts, though they bagged around her knees. She looked young and sexy and delightfully gamin.

"Sir! You can't go in with the lady!" Misty and Alan both ignored the clerk's scandalized tones.

"This," Misty said several minutes later, "is fun, too. I had no idea how much fun buying clothing could be."

Alan kissed her wrist as it emerged from the full, pleated sleeve of a silk blouse with a low-cut front and a nipped-in waist. She liked the way that particular shade of pink reflected in her cheeks. She couldn't have done better herself, she decided, and pulled on tight-fitting pants. As she tucked in the blouse and zipped up the front of the pants, Alan ran his hands over her hips.

"But then, you're an unusual woman, Misty. I can't believe you've never been shopping before."

"Why would I shop when I could make all I needed?"

"To give some lucky man the pleasure of helping you choose," he replied, grinning at her reflection in the long mirror. He sat behind her on a bench, holding a mountain of clothing on his lap. The garments they'd selected hung on a rod at the left of the small room. The rejects, very few, hung on the right. "To say nothing of the pleasure of helping you try them on."

It was their third store since breakfast, and Misty now owned everything from lingerie to casual wear, to suits and dresses and coats and shoes, though she could have done without the latter. At first, she'd protested. "But I have no money, Alan. You need money to get things in stores. Even I know that."

"You don't need money. Your things were lost through my negligence, therefore I will replace them. Now, don't argue. My insurance will cover it."

At last Misty convinced Alan she had more supplies than any two women could need for the next several lifetimes, and he consented to quit. For that day at least. "I'm sure you'll discover things we've forgotten," he said as they left the cosmetics department of a large store. "I like shopping with you. If you're not too tired, we need to replace everything that was taken from the kitchen, too."

He scowled as he opened the passenger door of his car for her. "I can't believe how little the thieves left us."

Misty waited until he was seated behind the wheel. "There were no thieves, Alan. I threw out everything when I first arrived. What I make is better. Was better. I'm sorry. I didn't know I'd lose my powers so abruptly."

She sniffed delicately. "I've caused you nothing but trouble."

He turned her face to his and kissed her gently. She read pity in his eyes, along with love, compassion. He still thought she was a crazy person, and loved her despite it. "You've given me nothing but joy."

"You won't feel terribly joyful when you discover I don't know how to cook."

He laughed and let his fingertips glide slowly from the back of her neck around her jaw and back to the steering wheel. He slipped the car into a break in the Sunday morning mall traffic. "Misty, you've already proven yourself a superb cook. It's too late now to pretend otherwise."

"But that was magic, Alan. That was before I became just an ordinary woman."

Parked in front of the supermarket, he drew her to him, kissed her until she was so dizzy she knew she'd stagger if she tried to walk. "My love," he murmured into her hair. "You could never be just an ordinary woman."

"Nevertheless, that's what I am."

"Good," he said, grinning as he opened the door. "I'm glad you're finally able to admit it. Come on, let's get some supplies, then go home for lunch. I want to see what kind of cook my suddenly 'ordinary' woman turns out to be. After all, even when we hire someone else to do the job, she's going to want days off. And quite frankly, cooking is not my strong suit.''

It's not mine, either, Misty would have liked to say, but maybe it would be. She didn't know. She'd never tried it the human way.

''MISTY, I DON'T LIKE this soup. It burns my mouth.'' It had a whole bunch of ice cubes in it and was pretty cold, but it still hurt Deanna's mouth.

''I know, powder puff.'' Misty looked really, really sad. ''It burns mine, too.''

''Can I have something else? A peanut butter sandwich?''

''Sure.''

Daddy came in then, and Misty whipped away the bowl of soup she'd put on the table for him, pouring it in the sink. ''It's terrible, Alan. Too much pepper.'' She sighed and shoved her hands through her hair. ''I'm hopeless! I'm useless! You'd both be better off without me.''

''No!'' Daddy's voice sounded too loud. His eyes looked funny. He grabbed Misty by the shoulders and held her in front of him. ''I won't let you leave me, Misty. Whatever this is that's bugging you, we'll work it out. Okay, so your cooking isn't up to standard. It was once—it will be again. In the meantime—'' He broke off, let her go and shrugged.

''In the meantime, you and Deanna starve.''

He laughed and kissed Misty loudly on the mouth. ''Not us, buttercup. Not as long as there's peanut butter in this world. Right, Dee?'' He picked her up and spun her around, then draped her across his shoulders with her head on one side and her legs on the other. He tickled her till she laughed, and then Misty laughed, too.

That made Deanna feel better.

They'd had peanut butter sandwiches for lunch yesterday, and the day before, too, but that didn't matter to Deanna. Misty could make those. And cheese sandwiches, but not grilled. She burned them.

She'd burned the potatoes last night, and the noisy 'larm in the ceiling went off. Daddy had come running, snatched the pot from the stove, flung it out the back door and then turned on all the fans to get rid of the smoke. It took a long time. Misty and Deanna had stood on the back porch with tears running down their faces, watching the rain come down.

Even after Deanna's eyes were all better, Misty's still cried. She cried harder when nobody's teeth could bite into the meat out of the oven.

Daddy had hugged Misty while she cried, then cooked bacon and eggs as she watched closely. Deanna liked it when Daddy hugged Misty and they both laughed, but that time Misty hadn't laughed. Misty didn't laugh much anymore at all, and she never wanted to play with Fairy-dog. He just lay there on Deanna's bed like a stuffed toy.

The next morning Misty put cereal into three bowls, then poured milk on until the cereal floated out. She put lots of sugar on. Deanna liked it, but Daddy sort of wrinkled his nose when he took his first bite and shoved his bowl away. "I think I'll make myself some toast. Anyone else?"

Deanna had some, with jam, but Misty just shook her head. Deanna saw she had tears in her eyes again, but she didn't let on. It made her sad to know Misty was sad.

"Can we go to the park today?" she asked after she'd finished her toast and juice.

Misty smiled and nodded, but it didn't look like a real smile. "Of course," she said, collecting dishes off the table and taking them to the sink. It took Misty a long time to do dishes now. She didn't just blink at them anymore like she used to, but put them in the dishwasher. She broke lots of them, and made Deanna wear shoes all the time now because there might be bits of glass on the floor.

"Can Fairy-dog come too?"

Misty said, "No," and Deanna wished she hadn't asked because she saw how sad it made Misty.

As they arrived in the park, she asked the question she'd been thinking all the way from home. "Misty, don't you want to be my elf anymore?"

To her dismay, Misty's face crumpled and she turned away, but not before Deanna could see she was crying again.

"Misty..." She tugged her elf's hand. Deanna cried, too. "Don't you like me? Did I be bad? Are you going to go away like my mommy did?"

Misty sobbed aloud while inside her something shattered. She gathered Deanna close, smelling her sweet little-child scent, needing no supernatural powers to recognize the depth of Deanna's hurt and uncertainty. "Oh, sweetheart, no, you couldn't be bad if you tried!"

"But are you going away?" Deanna's voice rose. "Are you, Misty? Are you?"

When Misty failed to reply at once, Deanna broke free and ran from her. "I'll tell my daddy!" she shouted. "He said you can't go! He said no, Misty. He did."

"Deanna, come back!" Misty raced after the child, but Deanna had a lead on her. Up the sidewalk she ran, toward the corner where she always got to push the button to make the light change, but she didn't stop, didn't push the button, and the light was red.

"No!" Misty screamed. She almost caught Deanna. Her hand brushed air by the child's back. A taxi rushed down the street, oblivious, as Deanna's flying feet left the curb, landed on the street. Misty concentrated, focused, gathered herself and—

Fell.

She went down hard, stunned by the magnitude of her failure, scrambled to her feet, saw the taxi bearing down on Deanna and launched herself into the air.

She dove across the path of the taxi, caught Deanna around the middle and rolled.

Tires screamed. Deanna screamed. Skin tore against rough pavement. Misty rolled, struck something hard with her shoulder. The taxi shot by in a black-and-white blur, then silence descended.

Into the silence came the sound of Deanna's wails. Misty lay on the street with her, held her, tried to soothe her, stroked her hair. Her hand came away sticky with blood.

Other people crowded around. Voices spoke. "If I didn't know better, I'd say the woman flew." "It looked like that to me, too." "Lady, are you all right?" "Let go of your daughter. Let me look. I'm a nurse."

Misty tried to comply. Her arms remained locked around Deanna. The voices went on, emanating from a circle of white faces bending over her. "That took guts." "I think she deserves a medal." "Look, they're both bleeding. Call an ambulance." The faces and voices swirled into a roar and Misty succumbed to a huge wave crashing over her.

ALAN STOOD at the window watching Misty and Deanna walk down the driveway. Deanna danced. She pranced. She bounced. He knew she chattered nonstop. Misty, who until four days ago had often seemed to float, now plodded. He felt the weight of her despair as if it hung over his own shoulders.

Why? What had gone wrong? Where had he failed her? Why was she so unhappy? All she would say about the matter was that she'd expected to spend the rest of her life as an elf, that she didn't know if she could adapt to life without magic.

Without magic? There was magic to spare, he thought, in their nights together. He believed she agreed with him in that. In bed, she came alive. In his arms, she was his Misty again, but with the light of each new day, she grew more and more morose. Should he take her to a doctor? Was she ill, or was it something else?

If only she would talk to him! Women talked, didn't they? They liked to examine every nuance and facet of a relationship, yet all Misty would say about theirs was that he made her very happy.

That, he knew, was a lie.

The last time she'd said it, he'd tried to kid her out of it. "Hey, I thought elves didn't lie."

Her purple eyes had gone as dark as night. Her mouth had drooped, and her head had hung low. "I'm not an elf," she'd said.

"Oh, baby, I know." He tried to comfort her with his words, with his arms, with his kisses. "I've always known that. But you're my love, my lover, and I want you to be my wife. Misty..." He'd lifted her head, peered into her drenched-pansy eyes and said, "Marry me."

He'd taken her passionate kiss as an affirmative reply, and their lovemaking that night had been especially poignant. To make love with his life's mate, he discovered, was different from anything he'd ever experienced. It was as if with each kiss, each touch, each stroke of their bodies together, they recommitted themselves to each other, renewed a pledge they had not yet spoken aloud.

With Misty and Deanna out of sight, Alan sighed and turned from the window. He sat before his computer, staring at the simulated galaxy on his screen, and didn't stir until the sound of an ambulance siren cut through his reverie. He frowned, tapped a key and brought his work in progress into being.

Work. Concentrate. Don't think. Things just had to get better.

MISTY CAME TO with someone picking grit out of her knee. "Deanna . . ."

"Your little girl's fine. You're in worse shape than she is. You rolled as you hit, a bystander said, and kept her from hitting the pavement."

"Her head. Blood."

The woman working over her lifted Misty's bandaged right hand. "Your blood. We thought it was hers, too, but she's fine. A smart little girl, too. She told us your phone number. Your husband's on his way."

"Alan? You called *Alan?*"

"Yes. Lie still. You can't sit up yet, I'm not—"

"Misty!" Deanna darted across the room to the edge of the table where Misty sat swaying back and forth. Someone lifted Deanna and put her beside Misty. They clung together. "Misty. I was scared. You had blood on you. Are you going to die?"

"ALAN, I THOUGHT she was going to die. I tried to save her and I couldn't! I can't stay! I can't! I'm no good as a nanny, no good as a human."

"Darling, you're a wonderful nanny. You'll make a wonderful mother. You'll—"

"No! No! You don't understand. I didn't know what to do. I tried to use magic, but my magic is gone. I couldn't make her safe."

"You could. You did. You saved her, Misty. Look, you're exhausted. You're hurt. We'll talk about this tomorrow. Sleep now. Please."

"Hold me," said the woman who had once been an elf. "Don't leave me."

All through the night, he held her. She awoke before he did and knew what she had to do.

Creeping from the bed, she slipped from the room, across the hall and sat on the edge of Deanna's bed.

"Good morning, powder puff," she said, stroking Deanna's hair back from her face.

Deanna smiled as she woke. "Misty, I had a bad dream."

"I know, darling. But it's over now. Deanna, I have to ask you to do something for me. It's important. I want you to say some very special words."

She coiled a pale curl around her forefinger. "I have to go away, Deanna. I must go back to the Upper World, but I can't do it without your help."

"Go away? Like my mommy?"

"Go away, but not like your mommy. In a different way. I'll still be here, love, still look out for you, but you won't see me."

"Where will you be?"

"I'll be close to you always, and I'll see you, even if you can't see me."

"Where will you see me?"

"I'll see you between waking and sleeping, between the morning breeze and the evening tide. I'll see you everywhere and everywhen all at the same time."

"Don't you want to be my elf anymore? Don't you want to be my nanny?"

"I'll always be your elf. But I can't be your nanny. I'm not good enough at it. I let you get hurt yesterday. I might let you get hurt again. I have to go home to the Mother of All and tell her I've failed again. Maybe she will forgive me for that, but if I let harm come to you, Deanna, I could never forgive myself.

"Now, will you say the words?"

"What words?"

"Elf of the Morning Mist, begone."

"And then you'll go?"

"And then I'll go."

"I don't want to say it."

"I know, darling. But there's no other way for me to go home to the Mother."

"Do you miss your mother?"

"Yes, Deanna."

"I missed my mother, but then you came. I love you, Misty."

"I love you, Deanna. I always will. And I'll watch over you forever."

"Like an angel? Like my mommy?"

"Exactly. But you must say the words."

Slowly, reluctantly, Deanna did. There was a little popping sound, a quick rush of air and then nothing but a tiny wisp of mist hovering over her bed.

She put back her head and yelled, "Daddy!"

Deanna huddled, weeping into the fabric of her toy dog. "What is it, baby? Did you have a bad dream?"

"No," she cried. "No, it was real. Misty's gone! She's gone home to the Mother of All. I can never see her again."

Without knowing how, Alan knew it was true. Misty had left sometime while he slept. There'd be no point in searching her rooms. The house, cold and vacant and hollow, echoed from her leaving, exactly like his heart.

He sat on the side of Deanna's bed, gathered her and the toy into his arms, held her on his lap and rocked her to and fro, to and fro, to and fro....

MOVING STEALTHILY, Alan opened Deanna's door and stood looking down at her. She slept curled in on herself, like a little fern not quite ready to unfold. The half-moon sliding out from behind a cloud cast a whitish light on her hair and he bent to touch the soft curls. This had been the first night in two weeks she hadn't cried when he put her to bed. It broke his heart to see her so unhappy, as unhappy as he.

But at least he could understand what had happened, why his life had been torn apart. Deanna was four years old. Such things went beyond her understanding.

The birthday party— He hated to remember the grim, joyless birthday party with his parents, a little girl Misty and Deanna had met in the park, the little girl's mother and him. Not much of a celebration, despite the balloons, the cake, the streamers and the party hats. He had it all on video tape, but it was a tape he knew he'd never watch. There were huge gaps in it, gaps he himself had caused by his inability to give Misty the acceptance she needed.

Each gap could have been filled by her shape alone, just as the gap in his life, in Deanna's, could be filled only by Misty. And he'd driven her away.

He found some comfort in his daughter's presence, even though she slept. Sitting beside her, he felt minimally less alone.

At last, though, he stood, and as he moved, a glint of silver on Deanna's bedside table caught his eye. A picture frame. Where had she gotten it, and whose picture did it contain?

Lifting it, hoping, almost praying, it might be Misty's image in the frame, he stepped back from her bed, eased out into the hall and pulled the door closed before turning on a light.

He stared, disbelieving, at the photo behind the glass. Pippa! Where had it come from? How— He recalled, shortly after she'd come, he'd said to Misty, *I wish I had a picture of her to give Deanna.* How had she made that wish come true?

A chill raced over his skin. He wished he hadn't asked that question, even of himself. He wished he could believe he'd taken the picture years before and forgotten it, and Deanna had found it somewhere. He could not. He knew that. Pip had had an almost pathological fear of cameras, not surprising now that he knew about her parents and the teachings of her childhood. Cameras were as strictly forbidden as were toys, which also shot down the idea that maybe it was one Pip's mother had given to Deanna.

Pippa's blue eyes stared back at him. Her hair shone gold, suggestive of what Dee's would be like when it was thicker, fuller, longer. Her smile was Deanna's—wide and generous and full of mischief—and he realized that, until that moment, he'd forgotten what Pip looked like. Sadness, affection, regret, all tugged at him as he gazed at the photo.

Then, silently, he reentered Deanna's room and replaced the picture. Before he could make his exit, she awoke. "Hi, Daddy."

Sitting down again, he brushed her hair back. "Hi, honey. I was looking at the picture of your mom. Where did you get it?"

"I think Misty gave it to me. On my birthday. It was there when I got up. My mommy was pretty, wasn't she?"

"As pretty as you are."

"I'm glad I had a pretty mom and a pretty elf. Daddy?"

"Yes, baby?"

"If I could wish for a elf and get one, how come I can't wish for a mommy and get one?"

"I don't know, Dee. Is that how you got Misty? You just wished for her?"

"I wished for a fairy, but the Mother of All didn't have any so she sent me Misty. I had to say, 'Elf of the Morning Mist, come to me,' and then she was my elf. Until she asked me to tell her to go away. I wish I hadn't told her that, but she was so sad, Daddy. Do you think she's happy now, in the Upper World?"

"I hope so, honey. Wherever she is, I hope she's happy." Then, feeling foolish, he said, "Dee? What would happen if you said those words again? Would Misty come back?"

She shook her head. "She can't. She can only come to each person one time. If they tell her to go away, she has to do that, then she can't come back. But she can see me."

"Can she see me?"

"Maybe. I think so. I think she can see anything she wants to see. Elves are magic."

He nodded. Deanna yawned. He snuggled her back down. "Go to sleep, baby. I'm sorry I woke you up."

"Tuck Fairy-dog in, too, Daddy."

Obediently, he stuffed the toy dog under the covers with Deanna and turned away. Out of the corner of his eye, he thought he saw the dog yawn, little pink tongue sticking out, sharp white baby teeth gleaming in the light from the hall. He whirled back, but all was still. Deanna slept. The toy was just a toy. After a moment, Alan left.

He went to his room, but not to sleep. He paced. The room confined him. He wrenched open the sliding door and paced outside, finding no relief even in the cool night air. "What have I done?" he whispered to the waxing October moon. But he knew. He'd taken from Misty all that made her unique, everything about her he'd learned to love. He'd denied her her true identity, and because she loved him, she had tried to make it work. His way.

Always, he'd wanted it to be his way. As if his way were the only right one. His hidebound beliefs had sent Misty away.

"Misty," he said in a whisper. "If Deanna's right, and you can see me, hear me, know this. I love you. I believe in you. I accept you for what your are."

No answer came. He sat on the cushionless wicker lounge chair and leaned back, hands behind his head, staring at the curdled clouds and the moon playing hide-and-seek.

He longed to reach out and touch Misty, ached to hold her, feel the silk of her skin and the resilience of her flesh, breathe the scent of her skin, bury himself in the honeyed hollows of her body.

"Oh, Misty, Misty, what do I have to do to get you back?"

There was no answer but the one in his mind, an echo of Deanna's telling him what to say.

He closed his eyes. He opened his mouth, but no sound came. He licked his lips, cleared his throat and, embarrassed by the foolish surge of hope that rose in his chest, squeezed his eyes shut and said, "Elf of the Morning Mist, come to me."

He felt a breath of warm wind come out of the cold, heard a faint popping sound and opened his eyes. A small circle of light glowed on the balcony railing. A whiff of sweet scent wafted over him, the scent of summer, the scent of phlox, the scent of love.

He didn't recall moving, but he was on his feet. He took a pace toward that light. "Misty?" The glowing light flickered, burned brighter, then flared into a brilliant slash of purple and an elf perched on the rail before him. She couldn't have been any bigger than a Barbie. Dressed in a short purple tutu kind of thing, she had curly purple hair, silver wings and bare feet. But he knew that face, knew those eyes, knew that voice.

"You called?"

Something suspiciously like a sob shook his chest. "Oh, Misty!" He held out his hand, she fluttered her wings and flew onto it. "Is it really you?"

"Of course it's really me. Who else would answer to my name? Really, Alan, it took you long enough. I'd given up hope that you'd call me, and was in the mi dle of a crash course on how to be a successful hun when you invoked me and popped me right out of class. The stars only know what the Mother will say."

"That's all I ever had to do? Say your name?"

"That's all. Oh. And you had to believe I'd come."

"Oh, Misty." He gave his head a slow shake. "If I'd only been able to admit earlier what I knew from almost the beginning, and didn't want to acknowledge, you never would have gone, would you?"

"No. I wanted to stay, Alan. I wanted it badly enough to try to do it your way. I'm sorry I was such a failure."

He held his hand closer and peered at her. "You? A failure? You did everything but rub my nose in the truth, but still I wouldn't see. And you know why?" He didn't wait for an answer. "Because I was so intent on proving to myself I could separate fiction from reality, I couldn't recognize the truth when I should have. I mean, you kept disappearing, for Pete's sake! And I made excuses for myself for not having seen you walk away. And the chocolate mousse. I know it wasn't on the table when you opened the kitchen door that night, yet before we sat down, there it was. The school bus, Misty. You moved it, didn't you? Twice!"

"Yes. I'm sorry I frightened you."

"Frightened?" He shuddered. "It still goes, you know. I don't want you behind the wheel of a car. Ever."

"Alan..." Reproachfully, she elongated the syllables of his name.

"Unless you promised not to use magic except in the most dire emergency. And it can't be an emergency you've created simply by driving like a lunatic. Understood?"

"Understood. Alan, you conjured me. I'm yours to command."

He grinned. "That's something a lot of men in the world would give a lot to hear from the lips of the woman they love, so I wonder why I'm having such a hard time believing you? I have a sneaking hunch you've got ways to make sure I never make a command you don't want to obey."

Misty sighed and fluttered her wings. "After all, Alan, it was me you called, not some wussy little fairy. If you didn't want an elf, you should have asked for something else."

His fingers curled up behind her in a protective barrier against the rising breeze. "I didn't want something else. I wanted you. Elf of the Morning Mist. Um, can you be like you were before? When I first saw you?"

Her nose wrinkled. "The green dress? The *shoes?*"

He laughed. "No. Let's try the purple gown and bare feet."

He heard a faint popping sound, felt another breath of warm air and Misty, his Misty, stood before him. Her waiflike brown hair appeared tossed by wind. Her pansy eyes shone. Her lips parted in a glad smile, and her arms encircled her neck as he grabbed her and held her tight.

"Am I really here?" she asked. "Are you?"

"Yes. Unless I'm dreaming." The taste of her kisses was no dream, nor was the sensuous feel of the silk gown as he smoothed his hands down her back. Her scent filled his nostrils, her voice murmured in his ear, and he broke from her, just far enough to look at her and assure himself she was real.

Something cold and wet pressed against his ank
Alan looked down. A brown-and-white puppy, w

gling all over, put its paws on Misty's purple gown and whined. She bent and scooped it up. "Fairy-dog! Where's Deanna?"

Deanna was right behind him. The wind whipped her nightgown around her feet. Alan lifted her up off the cold deck. "What are you doing out of bed?"

"Misty's home! Misty's home!" Deanna flung herself out of her father's arms and into Misty's. She and the puppy made a pair of wiggly armfuls. "Fairy-dog barked and told me. Oh, Misty, how did you come back?"

"Your daddy called me."

"And you came?"

"And I came."

"You're not going to go away again?"

Misty shook her head. "Not unless Daddy tells me to go. I'm his elf now, Deanna. He's the only one who can make me leave."

Alan encircled them both with his arms. "That," he said, "is something I'll never do."

"Oh!" Deanna said, pointing toward the sky. "What's that?"

"That's a celebration for us," Misty answered. "The Mother has sent an aurora."

Misty made a cushion for the wicker lounge, then she, Alan, Deanna and Fairy-dog snuggled together under a blanket of softest down. Overhead, the elves and fairies carried their torches over the waves of heaven. Up, down and around they went, circling the earth and sun and all the moons and planets, drawing big, wide bands of light that shimmered and shivered and swayed among the stars.

"Listen," said Misty. "Can you hear the angels sing?"

They listened, and they heard, while deep within, the voices of their hearts rose in song as well, rejoicing in the power of their love.

Merry Christmas, Baby!

A romantic collection filled with the magic
of Christmas and the joy of children.

SUSAN WIGGS, Karen Young and
Bobby Hutchinson bring you Christmas wishes,
weddings and romance, in a charming
trio of stories that will warm up your
holiday season.

MERRY CHRISTMAS, BABY! also contains
Harlequin's special gift to you—a set of
FREE GIFT TAGS included in every book.

Brighten up your holiday season with
MERRY CHRISTMAS, BABY!

Available in November at
your favorite retail store.

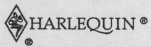

MC

1997
Reader's Engagement Book
A calendar of important dates
and anniversaries for readers to use!

Informative and entertaining—with notable
dates and trivia highlighted throughout the year.

Handy, convenient, pocketbook size to help you
keep track of your own personal important dates.

Added bonus—contains $5.00 worth of coupons
for upcoming Harlequin and Silhouette books.
This calendar more than pays for itself!

 Available beginning in November at
your favorite retail outlet.

The collection of the year!
NEW YORK TIMES BESTSELLING AUTHORS

Linda Lael Miller
Wild About Harry

Janet Dailey
Sweet Promise

Elizabeth Lowell
Reckless Love

Penny Jordan
Love's Choices

and featuring
Nora Roberts
The Calhoun Women

This special trade-size edition features four of the wildly popular titles in the Calhoun miniseries together in one volume—a true collector's item!

Pick up these great authors and a chance to win a weekend for two in New York City at the Marriott Marquis Hotel on Broadway! We'll pay for your flight, your hotel—even a Broadway show!

Available in December at your favorite retail outlet.

NEW YORK
Marriott®
MARQUIS

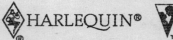 

NYT1296-I

HARLEQUIN®

Don't miss these Harlequin favorites by some of our
most distinguished authors! And now you can receive a
discount by ordering two or more titles!

HT#25657	PASSION AND SCANDAL by Candace Schuler	$3.25 U.S. ☐ $3.75 CAN. ☐
HP#11787	TO HAVE AND TO HOLD by Sally Wentworth	$3.25 U.S. ☐ $3.75 CAN. ☐
HR#03385	THE SISTER SECRET by Jessica Steele	$2.99 U.S. ☐ $3.50 CAN ☐
HS#70634	CRY UNCLE by Judith Arnold	$3.75 U.S. ☐ $4.25 CAN. ☐
HI#22346	THE DESPERADO by Patricia Rosemoor	$3.50 U.S. ☐ $3.99 CAN ☐
HAR#16610	MERRY CHRISTMAS, MOMMY by Muriel Jensen	$3.50 U.S. ☐ $3.99 CAN. ☐
HH#28895	THE WELSHMAN'S WAY by Margaret Moore	$4.50 U.S. ☐ $4.99 CAN. ☐

(limited quantities available on certain titles)

AMOUNT	$
DEDUCT: 10% DISCOUNT FOR 2+ BOOKS	$
POSTAGE & HANDLING	$
($1.00 for one book, 50¢ for each additional)	
APPLICABLE TAXES*	$_____
TOTAL PAYABLE	$_____

(check or money order—please do not send cash)

To order, complete this form and send it, along with a check or money order
for the total above, payable to Harlequin Books, to: **In the U.S.:** 3010 Walden
Avenue, P.O. Box 9047, Buffalo, NY 14269-9047; **In Canada:** P.O. Box 613,
Fort Erie, Ontario, L2A 5X3.

Name: _____

Address: _____City: _____

State/Prov.: _____ Zip/Postal Code: _____

*New York residents remit applicable sales taxes.
 Canadian residents remit applicable GST and provincial taxes.　　HBACK-OD3

Look us up on-line at: http://www.romance.net

Free Gift Offer

With a Free Gift proof-of-purchase
from any Harlequin® book, you can receive
a beautiful cubic zirconia pendant.

This stunning marquise-shaped stone is a genuine cubic
zirconia—accented by an 18" gold tone necklace.
(Approximate retail value $19.95)

Send for yours today...
compliments of HARLEQUIN®

To receive your free gift, a cubic zirconia pendant, send us one original proof-of-purchase, photocopies not accepted, from the back of any Harlequin Romance®, Harlequin Presents®, Harlequin Temptation®, Harlequin Superromance®, Harlequin Intrigue®, Harlequin American Romance®, or Harlequin Historicals® title available in August, September or October at your favorite retail outlet, together with the Free Gift Certificate, plus a check or money order for $1.65 U.S./$2.15 CAN. (do not send cash) to cover postage and handling, payable to Harlequin Free Gift Offer. We will send you the specified gift. Allow 6 to 8 weeks for delivery. Offer good until December 31, 1996, or while quantities last. Offer valid in the U.S. and Canada only.

Free Gift Certificate

Name: _____

Address: _____

City: _____ State/Province: _____ Zip/Postal Code: _____

Mail this certificate, one proof-of-purchase and a check or money order for postage and handling to: HARLEQUIN FREE GIFT OFFER 1996. In the U.S.: 3010 Walden Avenue, P.O. Box 9071, Buffalo NY 14269-9057. In Canada: P.O. Box 604, Fort Erie, Ontario L2Z 5X3.

FREE GIFT OFFER
084-KMFR

ONE PROOF-OF-PURCHASE

To collect your fabulous FREE GIFT, a cubic zirconia pendant, you must include this
original proof-of-purchase for each gift with the properly completed Free Gift Certificate.

084-KMFI

Now's your chance to get the complete
HERE COME THE
GROOMS™
series!
Order any or all 12 of these great titles:

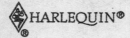 

You're About to Become a

Privileged Woman

Reap the rewards of fabulous free gifts and benefits with proofs-of-purchase from Harlequin and Silhouette books

Pages & Privileges™

It's our way of thanking you for buying our books at your favorite retail stores.

PROOF OF PURCHASE LL-PP19

Offer expires March 31, 1997

Pages & Privileges ™

Harlequin and Silhouette— the most privileged readers in the world!

For more information about Harlequin and Silhouette's PAGES & PRIVILEGES program call the Pages & Privileges Benefits Desk: 1-503-794-2499

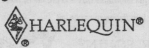

HARLEQUIN®

LL-PP19